STRANGE CONNECTIONS

G E WASHINGTON

Edited by: Audrey F Liggins

ISBN-10: 0-6157-8900-5
EAN-13: 9780615789002

TABLE OF CONTENTS

A DEAD BODY

Something clicked as I walked into room 205. My mind recognized the familiar scent as if I had been in this room before. It was a musky, aromatic scent of jasmine and sandalwood; deep and sticky, like dark honey. I knew that scent, had known it for over ten years; a scent that would remain on my body for a week, not wanting to wash it away because I wanted to smell him, remember him, keep him near. Yet tonight it was foul and made my stomach ache; the combination of body fluids and cologne. The odor was so foul that I prayed someone else smelled it, and I was just remembering. Remembering a time long ago, when he was good, and kind, and loving. Tonight it made me sick, sick to my stomach. Tonight it was more than a familiar memory; it was death.

As I glanced around the room, attempting to adjust my eyes to the sights before me, it became clear that something was very wrong. The two bodies lay one on top of the other in a gruesome display of missionary sex. The large man on top was naked except for a pair of blue socks. The female beneath him was not as large, but her body appeared to be lifeless and flattened. I wasn't sure if the weight of the body on her had caused the flattened form, or if she was just very thin. She looked odd. I walked over to the bed. The body beneath the man was a doll.

The owners of the motel called the police after several complaints from the other guests. One guest in particular went to complain because, he said, the noise was preventing him from getting high and he had spent good money on his crack and the crack whore who was keeping him company. Something, he said, had to be done. He couldn't get high and, if he didn't get his money's worth, someone was going to reimburse him. Most guests didn't complain since they didn't really want anyone to know they were spending time at the Star Inn. The Inn wasn't exactly a 4 star hotel; you wouldn't find it listed on Hotels.com or Hotwire. Most guests rented their room by the hour, or for a few hours. No one really spent the night there and, if they did, they didn't mean to. Loud music and arguing were a part of Friday night at the Inn, but this night something was different. The music wasn't loud, but the sounds were odd and continuous. Most guests at the Inn minded their own business, or at least they were too high to mind anyone else's. So when the music in room 205 never ended, something had to be done.

The police received the call around two a.m. and arrived at the motel ten minutes later. Yellow tape was placed around the door of room 205 and the cars parked in front of it. The remaining guests had been instructed that they should not leave until everyone had been questioned. Most guests were drunk so leaving was not an option. Others were too high and driver's licenses were scarce, if not suspended. No one offered any resistance. Things like this rarely happened at the Inn, usually people rented their rooms by the hour and after the crack was gone, so were they. No one used the rooms to sleep; sex maybe, and a quick nap, but no deep sleep. No one dared to spend the night. There were Jones' and Jacksons, Browns and Williams', but no first names. License plates were never accurately recorded, and no one paid for more than a couple of hours. The only way anyone stayed longer is if they had more dope. If you were still there when the sun came up you were in trouble, either with a wife or girlfriend or an angry husband. But no one ever came looking for you at the Inn. Most regular people only knew of its existence because they passed it on their way to work; never looking directly at it, just knowing that it was there because it was the only building along the stretch of highway that led into the city. Thirty years earlier it had been a very nice place to recommend to your friends when they came to visit. When crack hit town, it became the place to buy, sell and use dope. It happened overnight, like something out of a nightmare. It just … *was*. No longer could the owners rent rooms to weary travelers. Instead, they rented to locals needing a place to smoke dope or a cheating husband who wanted a blowjob but couldn't imagine doing it in his car parked along a deserted street.

The Inn was now covered in yellow tape, with blue police cars and flashing red lights. The owners, Mick and Rasheeda, were co-operating as much as they could. When asked about the occupants in room 205 they provided the type of car and a description of the man who got out to rent the room. He was tall, large, and very strong-looking. He was dark, and dressed in jogging gear. Mick remembered the logo on the jacket was Nike because he had one just like it, had gotten it at Macy's, "Clearance rack," he pointed out. The car was an SUV, probably a Chevy Equinox, he thought. Rasheeda remembered better since she had been bugging Mick to buy her one. “Black,” she said, “nice wheels, license plate Psalm 141:4.” Detective Peoples thought about this; who puts a bible verse on their car and spends time at a seedy motel?

The license plate came back as belonging to Michael Groves, pastor of the Greener Pastures church. Groves was the fourth pastor of Greener Pastures in less than three years. The church had been plagued with scandal for the last five years, ever since the elder Groves had passed away. It had also fallen on hard times, with each pastor embezzling more than the one before. Everyone in town knew about Greener. Some called it ‘Greedy Pastures’ due to all the corrupt and thieving pastors leading its congregation and the amount of money they had stolen. The elder Groves had built the church from the ground up. Most argued they’d actually seen him break ground with his shovel and remembered how he’d saved a small amount of dirt and had it made into a locket he wore around his neck on a gold chain. His wife had made sure he was buried with it when he died. Some people speculated that it hadn’t been dirt from the groundbreaking but rather dirt from the grave of his rival, a preacher named Huber.

Groves and Huber started out as friends back in the 60’s. They had attended the same high school in Birmingham, Alabama and had migrated to Kansas City in the early 70’s. Back then, the dream was to be top basketball players like Oscar Robinson or Wilt Chamberlain. Both men stopped dreaming when they realized they were just mediocre players and the only way they would be part of a professional team is if they owned it. So in the mid 70’s they decided to start a church, after attending a revival and noticing the amount of money people were willing to put in the collection plate. Night after night, they witnessed mothers and fathers with small children who barely had enough to eat put their hard-earned money in the basket.

Groves was the first who decided being a pastor was the way he'd make his fortune and become a millionaire. He decided he'd attend church, learn from the pastor and then after, say, three years, he'd take over. So he started out as a deacon of Christ Resurrected Church on Prospect and soon became an assistant to the pastor. He made himself available at all times, driving the pastor's big Cadillac and attending all church services day or night. Whenever the pastor was called, Groves was there. If a mother was distraught over her cheating husband and needed counseling, he would drive the pastor and wait outside while the pastor offered counseling and prayer. Sometimes the counseling took an hour other times it took a couple of hours. Each time the pastor emerged from the house he'd say, "The words of another man's wife may seem sweet as honey, they may be as smooth as silk, but in the end she will bring you sorrow."

Groves would smile and secretly wonder just how much time was spent counseling and how much time was spent screwing. It didn't matter because he was just biding his time, learning all he could from the pastor and waiting, waiting until the time was right when he'd use everything he witnessed against him. Each time he and Huber got together, he shared all the dirt he had on the elder pastor and say he was waiting for the right time to make his move. He was sure, he'd say, that if the church knew exactly what was going on he'd be in line to take over and when the time was right, he'd be ready. He would not make the same mistakes. He would not be weak to women and didn't understand how any pastor would allow sex to ruin a great gig like being a pastor. He had big dreams, bigger than anyone had seen or heard of, and chasing women would not get in his way. So he continued to drive and keep his mouth shut, secretly recording everything in his mind, making mental and sometimes written notes in his journal, anticipating the time when he would present all the dirty evidence to the church board. And then he'd step right in. One Sunday evening he requested a meeting with the deacons of the church, prepared to air all the dirt he had assembled on the pastor, when he noticed Huber in attendance. The two men greeted each other, and Groves asked Huber why he hadn't told him he was coming? Huber smiled and said he hadn't really planned on coming but that he'd been invited by one if the deacons. Groves was somewhat surprised to see him since he had been the one requesting the meeting with the senior deacons, and he had no clue who Huber knew and why he was there...

Huber had not been involved in the daily workings of the church; instead he had completely focused on seminary school. He decided he would not pursue a church until he had finished his degree. He'd always thought education was more important and he wanted to be ready when he was called. As the men gathered in the conference room Huber and Groves sat on opposite sides of the long table. The pastor sat at the head and four deacons each sat on either side of the table. The senior deacon, named Jones, started to speak. He told of adulterous liaisons with certain women of the church and monies that were unaccounted for. He spoke about church conventions where rooms were charged on the church's credit card, yet no one from the church had actually attended. He brought out copies of the church's credit card statement that showed several charges by a company called Don's Chiropractic, yet they couldn't find an address or phone number. Also, no one had any idea that the pastor suffered from a bad back. Altogether, more than $30,000.00 was missing or unaccounted for, and it all seemed to be traced to the pastor's credit card. When presented with the accusations, the pastor begged for forgiveness saying he was sinful and sought redemption from the church. Groves sat, smiling on the inside, thinking his job had been done for him, that he would soon be announced the new pastor of Greener Pastures and no one would know he had been preparing for such a role by exposing the former pastor. As the elders sat around the table, Jones finally stood and announced they had decided on someone who would take over the church. He spoke about having someone with vision, youthfulness, someone who was prepared to lead them. Then he stood … and introduced Huber as the new pastor of Greener Pastures. Groves slumped in his chair as he let out a deep, pained sigh.

Detective Peoples stood at the door and looked around the room. Nothing seemed to be out of place. Clothes were strewn on the floor. The Nike jogging outfit was laid out across the one chair in the room. The clothes on the floor belonged to what at first appeared to be a woman, but on closer inspection was a doll. It was life-sized, with long dark hair and round breast. The rest of the doll lay squashed beneath the man's heavy body. Peoples instructed the uniformed cops to stay outside while he began to look for clues and the medical examiner was called. Nothing was touched, but the sound was getting more and more annoying. In the corner next to the bed was a radio with a CD player. The CD appeared to be stuck because it was repeating the same song over and over and over again. The forensic team took photographs of the bodies on the bed and dusted for fingerprints on every visible surface.

Clothes were bagged, and anything that wasn't nailed down was put in paper bags for evidence. Finally, the body was examined for cause of death. On first examination, the body looked exhausted yet rested. The dead man was just beginning to turn cold and blue. He looked as if had been dead for over 3 hours. As the body was placed in a body bag and transported to the morgue, Peoples looked over at the bed shaking his head in disbelief at the sight before him. The body on the bed was beginning to come back to life. The air in the doll's flattened body was now filling the plastic form and once again gave the look of a real woman. Peoples looked at the plastic form and a breathed a sigh of relief. He was amazed, and wondered why any grown man would use a doll for sex and bring it to a hotel room. It didn't make sense. Moreover, he thought it was crazy because the man whose lifeless body being driven to the morgue was married to a very beautiful woman. Peoples should know, since he had dated the man's wife for three years and had never really gotten over the fact that she had married someone else. A doll, a scratched song on a CD player and hot Friday night .....This was only the beginning!

Peoples wasn't the friendliest man. He wasn't the best brother, or son, or boyfriend. What he was, was a very good detective, and if you happened to find yourself dead alone in a seedy motel with no clues as to who killed you, then you'd want him on your case. He was sometimes crude, and even rude. He didn't have much need for Diplomacy; he felt that was better left for diplomats. He felt everything he ever needed in life he learned in grade school. He lived alone with his dog, 'Stank', a pit bull/mastiff mix, with a brown brindle coat and a big sad face. Stank weighed over 120lbs and hated to get out of the bed. He slept most of the day except when Peoples would take him for their nightly ride around the neighborhood. Everyone in Peoples' neighborhood knew he was a cop and, although he wasn't over the neighborhood watch program, everyone felt safer when he was on duty, they all slept better too. Stank didn't like taking walks but preferred to ride much as he could. So every night, no matter what time he ended his shift, Peoples and Stank rode through their neighborhood. They also rode through hers.

He should have married her, he should have gone to college, he should have been nicer to the cashier at Price Chopper … he should have, etc., etc. He should have, but he didn't. He let her get away. He let her marry some idiot who didn't know his ass from a hole in the ground. He let her be unhappy with a man whose only purpose in life was to mess up. He let her live her life without him. Instead, he rode through her neighborhood each night, hoping to catch a glimpse of her through the window, doing what women do at night. He waited and watched, staying just a little too long outside her house one night, and he saw her … saw what women do at night when they're married. He saw her make love to her idiot husband … wishing it was him. But he was too full of himself and his 'it doesn't matter' attitude to do anything about it, so he drove on.

Lang Peoples had lived his whole life in Kansas City. He graduated from South East High in 1982. He worked with his father doing home remodeling until one day when he'd met a detective from the Kansas City Police Dept. They were there to remodel a bathroom, but instead he listened as the detective talked about what it meant to be a real detective, not like the ones on television. He was hooked. The detective told him about solving crimes, crimes that Peoples knew about through the news. He told Peoples how catching bad guys always gave him a rush and when the bad guy was locked up, he knew he had made the streets of Kansas City just a little safer. Peoples was young and awestruck, and knew at that moment remodeling was not in his future, he told his dad just that. But catching bad guys, now that was good stuff! He had all the time in the world for laying carpet, painting walls and hammering nails … but to track down a bad guy who thinks he's smarter than you, now that was just too exciting!

He had never been athletic and playing basketball or football was not a part of who he was. His brother John was just the opposite. He was the perfect jock. Tall, chiseled and fast, his brother played football, basketball and even baseball. He also had several girlfriends, unlike Lang, who had none. John was not as smart as Lang, but what he lacked in smarts he made up for in pure physical talent. The two brothers were as different as night and day. John grew to be 6"5 like his uncle Bob, while Lang stood around 6'. Both were solidly built like their dad and enjoyed hunting like he did. Their mother was the educated one in the family, having obtained both a bachelor's and a master's degree in psychology; she worked for a major telecommunications company as Director of Human Resources. Dad worked with his hands and his heart. Remodeling was what he did; helping people was what he loved. Neither son went to college. John, who everyone thought would be a professional athlete, met a girl from St Louis and married her. He moved to a suburb outside of St Louis, had three girls, and worked for a utility company as a lineman. Lang became a police offer and after ten years made detective. He loved his job. He was good at catching criminals and saw each case as a way to help keep his town safe. At least that's what he told everyone, but what really drove him was outsmarting criminals. He liked to battle wits, to out-think, to trip up his opponent; to be the victor. He secretly thought of himself as a General. Only one other person knew that: her, and whenever she wanted something from him she'd call him that.

She never called him that in public, only in private. She also loved him and wanted a life with him, but he was too afraid and too selfish to commit.

She wanted a husband, a stable life; he wanted passion and no commitment. So they did what they did best whenever they got together; they made love and pretended that one day they'd be together, once he was ready. He never got ready, so she married the idiot.

The story about the dead body found in the motel didn't make breaking news on any channel. Even Channel 5 with its live, late breaking news only showed the motel after all the police cars and traffic left. No sensational headlines graced the Kansas City Star; the only news media that seemed to care was radio station 107.3. That may have been because one of the major disc jockeys on the air belonged to Greener Pastures. Talk around town, though, was buzzing. Nieces was the place to be to hear anything about a case. If you had an opinion, it was accepted there and you almost always had a captive audience. Although you might be challenged by one of the regulars who of course knew everything that went on in KC, you would be encouraged to voice your opinion. Bad or good, right or wrong, everybody was a critic and everybody knew who did it. Some felt the wife did it. As old man Johnson said, "The wife is always a suspect and you can best believe the police are looking at her right now." "Nah, nah, nah," Jenkins said, "The wife didn't do it, 'cause she didn't have a motive. It wasn't like he was cheating with a real woman, he had a doll in the bed with him, and he wasn't the breadwinner in the family, she was. Nah,

I don't think she did it, I think they're gonna find out it was some serial killer, you know, some serial killer who got a thing against preachers. Hell if it wasn't for the fact that I'd go to hell, I'd kill me a preacher. Did I ever tell y'all about that preacher I almost killed back when I lived in Mississippi?" "Yes!" they all chimed in. "Yeah, and we don't want to hear it again!"

Peoples sat in his booth drinking coffee and listening to the group. He had learned long ago that to help solve crimes you had to be around the people. Most criminals liked to talk and brag and somebody who wasn't supposed to hear the conversation usually did. Then they'd tell their friend who'd tell his friend who'd tell his wife, who'd share it at the beauty salon and before you knew it a suspect would emerge, so Peoples sat … and listened.

A TALE OF TWO PASTORS

A phone rang inside a small apartment filled with bags and bags of trash. The windows were filthy from cigarette smoke residue and the kitchen faucet dripped. Old magazines and food ads covered the coffee table. The living room was full of the type of old, discarded furniture usually found dumped alongside the road. A large, overstuffed brown recliner and a torn, cat-stained ottoman took up most of the room. The couch was the color of wine and smelled of it as well. A phone lay on the floor beside a bed covered with a ripped comforter and no sheets. The bed had been pushed against the wall since there was no headboard, with a battered mattress on its frame only inches off the floor. The bedroom had no chest or drawer for clothes. Just bags, yellow trash bags of clothes were in every corner of the room. The phone rang and then went silent. Minutes later, it rang again. Someone wanted to get in touch with the person who lived there, except no one was home. The phone went dead, and then it rang again. This time the caller let it ring once before hanging up and calling back.

Peoples went to the station to work on the Groves case. No leads had come in, but no crazies were claiming to be the murderer either. The cause of death was still unknown so everyone was busy concentrating on older cases. Peoples started compiling a list of family and friends who knew the younger Groves and at the top of the list was *her*, Mrs. Groves. He smiled as he wrote her name on the paper realizing that he would get a chance to talk to her and to see her. No more drive by's wishing he'd catch a glimpse of her; soon he'd call her to arrange a meeting. Of course he wouldn't ask her to come to the station, no, he wanted to see her where she would be most comfortable and where he wished he lived with her. He wanted to finally see the inside of the house he drove past every night.

All the years he drove by during his neighborhood watch, he never went inside her house, imagining, instead what he thought it would look like. The kind of furniture he knew she liked, what color the walls were and what kinds of paintings she had on them. Had she displayed any of his? He had done two for her back when they dated: one was of a little girl on a porch; the other one was of her beloved dog, Suga. He wondered if she'd told her husband where the paintings had come from. Had he known about them, or had she told him they were bought at a flea market instead? Whatever the case, soon he'd be inside her house, standing close to her, smelling her and wanting to hold her.

The city moved along quietly. Neighbors barbecued on Saturdays and went to church on Sundays. Life was on schedule. It was July in KC and Swope Park was full of concertgoers. All the top R&B singers made their way to KC, usually stopping in St

Louis first and then moving west. This summer the list of entertainers provided something for everyone. Young or old, hip-hop to jazz, Broadway or off-Broadway, no one was left out. The city was full of things to do. The plaza was the background for many summer weddings. It was nothing to see five or six wedding parties' parade down JC Nichols Parkway. Beautiful brides and handsome grooms in horse-driven carriages kissed and danced the night away. Promises of love forever, through good and bad, sickness and health gave young love hope. No one ever dreams of cheating spouses, annoying in-laws, down-low husbands, unruly children or job loss. No marriage ever prepares for divorce, or wants to share stories of infidelity in divorce court. Some KC residents found themselves on Maury anyway, because they couldn't figure out who the daddy was. For some, anything that took away the pain was worth doing. The inner city was dying. The older generation refused to move to Lee Summit or Raymore, but their children did. Higher incomes afforded some with homes they had only dreamed about. Many worked for Sprint or Ford, or made their livelihood in the medical field. Doctors, lawyers, teachers, the educated masses left the city and moved to the suburbs. Most people felt if they left the inner city, they'd leave the bad things behind. Somehow, the city followed.

Peoples was called out to a domestic disturbance between two men. The men were each holding knives, threatening to cut the other one. One was tall and slim with skin the color of copper, the other one was dark and short and had a round belly, fully exposed and inches away from receiving a deep stab wound. The men were both loudly accusing the other of cheating. Neighbors on each side had come out of their houses to see the confrontation go down. The men lived in the neighborhood for over thirty years and had been with each other for just as long. Most neighbors had witnessed the loud arguing before, but this time was different. This was the first time either had brought a weapon. The verbal assaults were very rude and full of sexual innuendo. Some of the neighbors pleaded with them to stop and go inside. Neither one would budge. One man stood on the steps and the other stood in the doorway to the home. The taller one, standing in the doorway, called the police. He was the one who pulled his knife first. The shorter one was not as verbal; he was on the steps leading away from the house. He refused to make a move toward his lover, just grunted words that were barely audible. When Peoples and his partner arrived, he recognized the shorter man and slowly walked toward him.

"Hey Lou, what's going on here man?" The man continued to grunt and stare at his lover. "What's the problem, guys?" Peoples asked. "Let's put down the knives so we can talk." The shorter man obliged, but the taller one continued to yell obscenities, telling Detective Peoples that he wanted the 'short son of a so-and-so' to get out of his house. Peoples told him that if he put the knife away, he'd put Lou in the police car and get to the bottom of things. The taller man did as he was told and sat in a chair on the porch. The second police officer put the shorter man in the squad car and started asking him what happened. Peoples ascended the steps and began talking with the taller man. "What's your name sir?" "Allen," the man responded. "What's going on here, why are you two threatening each other?" "'Cause I'm tired of his lying and cheating ass, every time I go out of town, he brings some bitch in my house and lays up with them. We been together for over thirty years and I have never cheated on him, but every time I leave, if just for a weekend, I find out some body has been in my house and in my bed, and the killing part is he brings *women* in here. He knows the only woman that can lie at my house is my mama, and she been dead for ten years. I don't play that! " "Well," Peoples said, "did you catch the woman in your house when you got back?" "No," the man said, "no, I didn't catch her cause if I had, you'd be taking me to jail for murder! No, I didn't catch them, he told me he let some woman stay at our house for two nights 'cause she didn't have anywhere to go. He is always rescuing somebody. He probably screwed her too." "Well," Peoples said, "I don't think that's reason enough to go pulling knives out on each other. Let me go talk to him and I'll be right back."

When Peoples reached the squad car, Lou was smoking a cigarette. It brought back memories of a different time. Peoples had been a two-pack-a-day smoker for ten years and when he quit he swore he'd never smoke again. He had a close call with lung cancer at the age of thirty-two and the doctors had warned him that between his job and the nicotine, he'd be lucky to live to be forty. He was now forty-six and cancer-free. Cigarettes were easy to let go, the job was not, it was his life and he'd do it until he died, or was physically unable to continue. Even then, he thought, if his mind remained sharp, he would teach at the academy. Catching bad guys was his passion, and he would never stop. The taller man on the porch leaned toward the railing to hear what was being said to his friend. "Now Lou, tell me what's going on, your friend there said you let some woman stay here while he was away, is that true?" "Yeah, I let her stay; she didn't have anywhere else to go. She was all right. She wasn't a dope fiend or thief or nothing. She just was down on her luck, said her old man had put her out and she didn't have a family here. I met her at the bus station when I was down there picking up cans. She asked me for $2.00 for a sandwich, so I told her I didn't give my money to people, but

I'd go get her a sandwich. So I went to the restaurant and got her some food. She ate it and then she asked me if I knew where she could sleep for the night. I told her she could try the mission, but I wouldn't really recommend it for women, so she asked if she could sleep at my house. She promised she would leave the next day. So I told her yeah. She looked okay. I brought her to the house; she took a bath, went to sleep on the couch and left in the morning. I don't know where she went after that: didn't even get her name. I tried to tell that fool up there what happened, but that nosy bitch next door beat me to the punch, so he got mad and started saying he was going to ' kill me…cut off my privates and all that old nasty stuff. I've been with him for over thirty years and I've never cheated on him. I love him, but I ain't going to let him cut me." Peoples sighed and then told Lou to come with him. They went up the stairs to the porch where the taller man was sitting and Peoples told him what Lou said. "I believe him too," Peoples said. "You two stop acting crazy and make up. I don't want to come back here tonight or any other night with the two of you fighting." The taller man looked at his partner, took his hand and smiled. "I'm sorry Lou. You know I love you and I have never let anybody in our house. I know Mrs. Long is always in our business, but I guess I just overreacted. I don't want to fight anymore." Lou looked at his partner and said, "That sounds good, now what you gonna cook, 'cause I'm hungry."

Peoples and his partner left the two and headed back toward the station. That was just like Peoples; he was never quick to arrest, because he hated the paperwork. But if things didn't get worked out, he'd work you out. He was known for hitting people when they were handcuffed. He was also known for how badly he talked to them, often calling them 'stupid', or 'downright dumb'. It was nothing for him to call people 'deadbeats', or 'trash', or tell them they deserved to be victims. Once he told a homeless man who had been robbed, that he should count himself lucky that he was already broke. He had little patience for people who lived a street life and felt justified in treating them that way. Several citizens had filed complaints against him, but never for extreme force. More often it was his rudeness and lack of empathy. The captain loved him, though, and nothing was ever done.

Peoples called the medical examiner to find out if there was any news about the Groves murder. It had been a little more than a week and, although he knew it was a homicide, the real cause had not been clear. He called the ME and told him he was on his way to get the report. He liked visiting the morgue, discovering the cause of death, unlike some of the other detectives who just wanted the facts. Peoples liked seeing and watching the medical examiner in action. When he was a detective of just one year, he had his first opportunity to watch an autopsy performed. He was fascinated, and hooked. It made him face the practical side of life, knowing that no matter how you lived your life, money or not, in the end everyone was equal. All dead bodies received the same treatment. He liked that and it kept him grounded. The medical examiner met Peoples in his office and began explaining in medical terms what he determined to be the cause of death. The cause of death was heart failure, he said. Groves had serious issues with his heart; it was enlarged and had several blocked arteries. He had been a time bomb ready to explode at any moment, the pathologist said. Medical records from Groves' primary physician had been requested and it determined there had been heart problems for some time. He had actually been advised to see a cardiologist and told to prepare to have an angioplasty. He had also been given a prescription and put on a special diet.

Peoples didn't like the sound of this, because it meant that whoever had been in the room with Michael Groves that night might not be responsible for his death and therefore no murder had been committed. More had to be done, something was overlooked. He would make sure the investigation would not end with notes from a doctor, a full and thorough investigation would be done, although he cared little about Groves. He wanted to solve the murder and since Groves had gone and gotten himself killed, bad heart or not, then he would solve it. Maybe he had a bad heart, but that wasn't the reason he lay dead in Room 205. If his heart had given out, then something or someone had triggered it and he would find out who did it. Catching bad guys, figuring out their next moves, triggered something inside him and made him good at his job. Peoples lived for the challenge, the mission to track and trap. He asked the doc if he could take the report back to the station because he was sure something was missing. The puzzle was not complete, and Peoples was good at puzzles.

Stank greeted his master at the door. He was so large he couldn't jump, so he lumbered toward him and laid his big head against Peoples' leg. A scratch behind the ears and a pat on the head completed the welcoming ritual between man and dog. Peoples walked through his house as he did every night, making sure nothing was out of place. Even though he had Stank, he never felt safe enough since he had been robbed three years ago. Right after that he got Stank. That night remained etched in his brain and the violation he felt was unforgettable. Everything had been turned inside out. Kitchen cabinets were broken and the contents spilled on the floor. A large television that normally resided in an entertainment center was gone and so was the entertainment center. All his CDs and DVDs were either stolen or broken. Books were strewn about the place and dirty dishes were in the sink.

After taking in the chaos in the living room he walked into his bedroom and went directly to the nightstand where he kept a small pistol. Although the standard firearm for detectives was the Glock-30 .45 sub-automatic, he'd always had a smaller Beretta .87 Cheetah inside the top drawer. It was missing. A few pieces of jewelry and a few dollars were also stolen. He figured it was some neighborhood kids until he found out six other residents had also been burglarized within the month. This alarmed him since most in the neighborhood knew he was a cop and even with that, he too had become a victim; so began his neighborhood watch. He walked through the house, pausing in every room to make sure things were in the same place as they had been when he'd left for the morning. Windows were still locked and all electronics seemed to be in place and in working order. He smiled at Stank and went to make a sandwich. As the smell of hamburger filled the air, Stank slowly emerged and headed into the kitchen. He looked up at Peoples and then down to his bowl, which was bone dry. Peoples smiled and went to cabinet to get his dog food. He filled the bowl with beef and liver-flavored canned food and mixed a little dry dog food with it. As the grease from the hamburger filled the skillet, Peoples took a little to the side and waited for it to cool. After making his sandwich, he poured some of the hamburger grease onto Stank's food, mixing it in. The dog devoured it in minutes.

Peoples propped himself up in bed and began reading the autopsy report. Blocked arteries and poor diet had supposedly caused Groves' fatal heart attack. He continued to read the primary physician's report: high cholesterol readings, elevated blood pressure and some notes indicating that Groves had complained of pain in his left arm. One night, Groves had been rushed to the emergency room complaining of shortness of breath. The hospital kept him there overnight for observation and the next day his doctor arrived to release him. The doctor told him to make an appointment for a stress test and a heart scan. The appointment validated all and confirmed the presence of heart disease. It was also noted that the heart disease was hereditary. His father and two uncles had had heart disease. Both uncles had died due to heart failure, but his father had died in a car accident. Some believed his father's rival, Huber, had staged the accident.

The elder Groves could never get over that day in church where all his dreams ended. When the deacon announced Huber as pastor of Greener Pastures, Groves became a hurt and wounded soul. The friendship between Huber and Groves was never the same, and so Groves set out to ruin Huber. Every chance he got; he would try to dig up dirt on Huber. He had spies in the church who posed as deacons but whose actual job was to report any and all mishaps to Groves. Huber performed well for the first three years until a young lady named Josephine joined the church. Josey was a beautiful woman whose father was from Nairobi and her mother from the Caribbean. She was tall, around 5'10" with curves in all the right places. She had the clearest skin with slanted hazel eyes. Some of the congregation thought she was half Asian and Black, but whatever they thought, they all agreed she was beautiful and so did Huber.

Josey joined the church on a hot Sunday afternoon and soon began her climb toward becoming first lady. She sang in the choir and created a single mother's ministry. Some of the elder mothers were against the ministry saying it condoned sex outside of marriage. Most were against it because she had come up with the idea, and anything she asked Huber to do, he did. When she wanted the choir to wear regular street clothes instead of robes; Huber granted her wish. When she requested the church sponsor a little league team, the church took money from the usher's annual picnic and pledged it for the softball team. What most suspected, but couldn't prove, was that most of these deals were worked out in Josey's bed. Huber was a virgin at forty years old and the closest he had come to actual sex was watching a soft porn movie one night when he was in seminary. Since the school taught against sex before marriage, Huber never watched another movie. After school he tried to date a young woman whose brother was his study mate. The night they went out, she had worn a sundress and no bra. She had developed a reputation for seducing seminary students and tonight was Huber's turn. They went to the movies and she sat with her legs crossed allowing her dress to rise above her knees, exposing tight, firm thighs. Huber tried to watch the movie while sneaking looks at her thighs. When the movie was over, she suggested they get ice cream and sit in the park. Huber obliged, being the perfect gentleman. When they found a bench to sit on, she planted herself so close to him that he began to sweat. She licked her ice cream as if she were performing in an adult movie. Huber asked her if she were a virgin, and she responded, "No. Why, are you?" He said, "Yes," and with that, they drove back to the school.

With Josey, things were different. He was older, and ready to know what it felt like to be with a woman. He was so attracted to her that he often appeared at every choir rehearsal, although before she came to the church, he never found interest in attending the choir's practice. He made sure he was always available for her; no request too minor for him to respond to and most of the time they met in his study. Of course Josey was no fool and knew the affect she had on him. Whenever she sang a solo, she would look directly at him, gazing intently; sending him into a trance.

One weekend the church traveled out of town to do a revival. Josey told the choir she would not be going because she had come down with a cold and couldn't really sing. The choir director told Huber about this, so after the choir finished practicing, he headed toward her house. When he was about a mile away, he phoned her asking if she was okay and if she needed anything for her cold. She told him that she thought he was real sweet, caring about her, but that it was just a cold and she had taken something. He told her that he was headed to the store and would buy her some orange juice and cough drops. She said that would be nice, but that it really wasn't necessary. He insisted. When he arrived at her door, she answered it in a thick white terry cloth robe. Her hair was down, and looked as if she had been rolling around in the bed. She apologized for her appearance and led him into the living room. He asked which way was the kitchen and headed in that direction as she sat down on the couch. When he returned, he had a big glass of juice and a box of tissues. He then found her bathroom where he wet a towel and told her to come and lie in her bed while he took care of her. He placed the towel on her forehead and told her to lie back. She did as she was told, but after about a half hour she began to sweat. He untied her robe and let it fall away from her body. Underneath she wore a sheer black nightgown with nothing on beneath it. She pretended not think about the fact that she was really naked, the gown was so sheer; it was like a film over her body. Her breasts were large and firm and her belly flat. He looked at her body and began to breathe deep. For a moment, he thought about closing her robe and leaving, but she caught his hand and placed it on her stomach. Then she looked up at him with those slanted eyes and all was lost. They made love twice, and after it was over, he told her that he didn't want this to be the only time they were together. He explained that if the church knew, he'd be forced out. The only thing left to do would be to get married, and so she began to plan a wedding.

Somehow, Groves got wind of the impending marriage and began asking everyone he knew what they knew about the wedding plans, but more importantly he wanted to know about Josey. What he found out only fueled his fire, and it gave him the ammunition he had hoped for to get rid of Huber. The deacon spies he had in the church never really produced any dirt on Huber, but finding dirt on Josey was a different story. Who knew his future would come in the form of a beautiful woman who herself had also been on a mission. He was overjoyed and anxious.

Although everyone agreed Josey was beautiful, what no one knew was that Josey had begun life as a male. She had been born Joseph and lived most of her early adolescent years as a boy. When Joseph was about eight years old, he told his mother that he was a little girl and no longer wanted to wear boys' clothes. His mother was surprised but loved her son with all her heart. She was also scared that he would be picked on and bullied, and since his father had left them, she feared what life would hold for them without a male figure in the picture. When he turned ten, they moved from the Caribbean to New York. Joseph began dressing like his girlfriends in the neighborhood and no one really knew any differently. Only the teachers at the school knew because he was listed as Joseph on his school records, but no one else. His mother would address him as 'Josey' and buy him clothes and jewelry. His hair grew long, and she had it done every week like her own. When he was 16, he began hormone treatments and his mother began saving for his sex-reassignment surgery. Josey took a job in a women's boutique where everyone accepted him and donated to his operation fund. When he turned twenty, he found a doctor to perform the surgery, and so began his life as Josephine. Life as a woman was wonderful and no one except for her mother and friends at the boutique knew how her life had begun. After becoming a woman, she modeled for a few years and went to college, where she earned a degree in business. Her mother became sick when she was twenty-five and died within a few short months. She decided to search for her father, but found the search to be futile. Her father had returned to Nairobi, gotten married and had five children. He would not respond to any of Josey's attempts to know him or allow her to know her siblings.

Josey met a man online who lived in St Louis, so she moved there and began living life fully as a woman. One night her lover invited her to attend a church revival. She had never attended church and had no sense of God or religion, but that night she felt moved in a way that made her want to know more, and she began to seek a place within the church. As she searched for a place where she could actively participate and not feel different, she landed at Greener Pastures. She wanted to be involved and felt the church was a safe place for her, though she knew she would never be able to tell anyone her secret. She saw herself as a First Lady, and she liked the sound of it. Most preachers were married, and trying to find an unmarried one was like looking for a needle in a haystack until she found Greener Pastures and its latest preacher; Huber. She moved to Kansas City, seduced Huber, and had began making wedding plans when Groves began scheming to have Huber removed.

Groves discovered medical records from hundreds of male-to-female transsexuals had been breached and were posted on the Internet. The doctor who performed the surgeries had been under investigation for Medicare fraud. Someone had hacked into his records and posted them on an internet site known for uncovering medical fraud. The name Joseph Paul appeared on the list. Groves didn't think much of it at first. Then he discovered information that said Joseph Paul had been born to a prominent political activist in Nairobi. No, he thought, strictly coincidence. Josey was all woman, and trying to make a case that she had been born a man was just too good to be true: surely his luck couldn't be that good. So he asked a reporter friend of his if he could look into it and let him know what he found. He told his friend that he was working on a sermon about homosexuality and other sins and wanted to add a little twist to his sermon. What his friend discovered gave him the proof he needed to get Huber removed and he was chomping at the bit to tell all.

He never confronted Huber or Josey, however. Instead, he went straight to the elders of the church. Groves once again assembled all the deacons together and this time he invited Huber. He got up and began to quote scripture on the abominations of homosexuality. He talked about fornication and sex before marriage. He talked about leadership and how some were behaving unethically. He said he had information that the pastor had been having an affair with a man and that he had actually begun planning on marrying him. Huber stood up and called Groves a liar. "I have never lain with man. What are you saying; are you really so bent on revenge that you would create lies like these to get me removed?" The deacons looked confused and shocked at the revelations being spewed by Groves. Then Groves handed a large manila envelope to the senior deacon. In it were pictures of Josey as Joseph. There were pictures of her and her mother at parties when she was a little boy, although dressed as a girl. There were also pictures of her as a woman in a bathing suit, an evening gown and sexy underwear taken when she was a model. Then there were pictures of Huber leaving her house on late nights and even one of them kissing and holding hands outside a restaurant.

Huber was sick with shock. He never spoke another word but silently left the church. He went straight to Josey's house and confronted her, she admitted everything but said that she really was a woman and was unashamed of anything she'd done. She told him that instead of running away, he should have stayed and defended her. She told him that he was stupid and should have recognized what Groves was up too. Everyone knew that Groves hated him and wanted to be pastor, he should have fought for his church and for her. She told him to get it together and think things through, because they had a wedding to plan. Huber looked at her and smiled. "You're right," he said, "I need to get it together" He went outside and got in his car. He drove back to the church. Everyone had gone, and the parking lot was empty. He sat in his car and turned on the radio, reached into the glove box and pulled out a small gun. Then he got out and went to the trunk of his car and got a folder. When he got back into the car, he entered on the passenger side and let the seat back as far as it could go. In the folder were pictures of Josey, as a little boy and as a grown woman. He had known for over a month, and had feared the worst. He placed the pictures on the driver's side and clutched one in his left hand. Then he pointed the gun to his temple, and pulled the trigger.

LOVE RECONNECTED

Groves became the pastor of Greener Pastures with Huber gone, and Josey began looking for another church.

Michael was the eldest of three children and the one most like his father. He hung on his father's every word and thought him to be the smartest man in town. Michael wanted to be like his father and never wanted to disappoint him. Whatever the elder Groves asked of him, he did without hesitation. When Michael was in grade school, he learned to play the trumpet because his father played it in school. When he went to high school he played football and baseball, because his father told him he should play and he had the skills to be the best. He also told his son, that what he lacked in brains, he made up for in brawn. Michael was the one who went to church every Sunday, without being reminded.

Going to church and staying out of trouble was expected of all the Groves children. For the most part, they abided by the rules set forth in the Groves house, and if they didn't they would pay for it. Michael aimed to please and he rarely disappointed his father. He received a full ride to a local university where he played sports and graduated with a degree in sociology. He was not a standout on the field, but on campus he was in hot demand. He was good-looking and humble. Most of the women loved him, but the guys thought he was a goody two shoes. He only dated a handful of girls, preferring to go home and be with his family any time he could. Dating and socializing on campus demanded too much of his time. In his senior year he met the one he would marry, the one who would walk into a sleazy motel room and see his dead body. Her name was Vhannie.

Peoples had fallen asleep when Stank's low growl awakened him. As he jumped up from the sofa, he remembered he had forgotten to make the neighborhood run. He put on his shoes, grabbed his service revolver and headed for the front door. As he opened it, Stank ran barking, growling and searching the grounds, looking for something or someone. Peoples didn't know what he was looking for, as he slowly began to walk around his car. With his gun aimed to shoot, he steadied his pace, walking confidently, without fear. Stank appeared at the end of the car, panting and growling. The dog hesitated for a moment, and then lumbered his way toward the passenger door and waited to be let in. Peoples looked down his driveway left and right, not seeing anyone, but feeling that someone or something had been watching him.

They got into the car and began their drive through the neighborhood. Lights were on in living rooms and along driveways. Some neighbors were sitting on porches, drinking and laughing, and eating leftovers from barbecues earlier in the day. Peoples drove on. When he got to her house, he slowed down. He looked in the front picture window where the curtains remained open at all times of the day or night. He hated that and wanted to tell her to buy some drapes or something to put up to that window. But then he thought if she did that, he would never be able to see her. And he wanted to see her, actually looked forward to seeing her. He looked in her window again, and realized she was looking back at him. He got nervous, but didn't move. She moved away from the window, and opened her front door. She walked out on the porch and sat on the swing. He hesitated in his car and started to get out, but he was too scared to move, so he drove on.

Where Peoples was direct and almost void of emotion, Vhannie was kind, sweet, and practical. She worked for a large bank as a manager after graduating with a bachelor's degree in psychology and a master's in finance. She was pretty, yet simple. She wore little makeup and dressed less to impress than she did for comfort. Her staff saw her as easy going but fair. Her political views tended to be conservative, yet she often cried when confronted with a sad story. She believed people should work hard and if so, then they could live the kind of life they wanted. She didn't believe in hand-outs, only hand ups. The one thing she loved to do was debate; any issue was okay with her. She loved it, and if friends attempted to debate her on social issues, the arguing could go on for weeks at a time, so most conceded the victory to her. Once she overheard her friends say she thought she was always right. Vhannie thought about it for a moment, then decided that she didn't think that way, it just happened that most of the time she *was* right. She worked hard and played little and after Michael's death, life had become dull and boring.

Her life had been centered on Michael until he died. She loved him and liked taking care of him. He was everything she wasn't, and they were committed to each other. She had waited years to get married, and had just turned 35 when Michael proposed. They met in college and dated for a while, but when he returned to KC to be with his family, she thought it was a mistake. She knew how much he idolized his father, and knew that when he returned, he would become his father's puppet. Vhannie never liked the elder Groves, or the church. She knew all the gossip about the elder Groves and Huber. She heard about the boy-turned-girl who brought the church down. She also knew Michael wanted to be like his father, and for that reason alone she had not followed him after graduation. Years later, she received a job offer to manage a branch office in KC and the pay was good. She decided to accept the offer, and once she arrived she made an effort to contact him. They began to date again and were engaged and married for over ten years. She also met Peoples.

One of her branches had been robbed on a busy Friday afternoon. The robbers had cased the branch for over month and decided on Friday the 13th to enter. With guns drawn, the robbers entered the branch looking for a big pay day. Vhannie sat at her desk preparing a report for the next day when the gunmen entered, telling everyone to hit the floor. Most people did as they were told; a few of the male customers grabbed their wives to protect them. The robbers were across the counter and in the teller drawers in seconds. She could only watch and pray that someone had pressed the silent alarm. One of the gunmen stood outside her door, watching her and making sure she didn't move. "Don't be a hero," he said. Vhannie sat motionless and watched in complete shock as they began to run out the door into parked cars. After the all clear sign was given, the doors were locked and she began to secure the teller line. The customers were asked to stay and fill out a description of the robbers or asked to leave their contact information if they couldn't or wouldn't stay. Within minutes, the FBI and KCPD arrived. .

The FBI dusted the counter for fingerprints, took tellers aside and got descriptions of the robbers. Teller drawers were counted to determine how much cash was stolen. The customers were shaken and a little afraid to leave, but most held up under the pressure. Families were called to say all was well. The local television stations' vehicles were everywhere. Passersby and gawking teenagers assembled outside the branch, either to be on the news or to just to be nosey. The local police and the FBI huddled together and asked questions of most of the staff. Vhannie began answering phone calls from bank security and vice presidents. Slowly, things were back to normal. The next day she was asked to visit the police station to see if she could identify one of the robbers. When she walked into the station she noticed him: Peoples was busy talking with another detective when he saw her. She smiled at him as he walked toward her with his hand outstretched. She shook his hand and gave him a hug. At that moment the past became the present. "How have you been Vhannie? She smiled and his heart melted.

In the cluttered and dirty room, the phone rang again...this time the occupant answered. While the caller on the other end demanded answers, the receiver said only, "Yes, yes, I know...no, no I didn't mean it." The occupant whispered into the phone as if there were others in the room and there was a need to keep the conversation secret. There was nothing to distinguish the room, except the smell of unwashed clothes and food left uneaten. Music played softly in the background on an iPod. The occupant remained calm and controlled as the speaker demanded to know what was going on, why the plans changed and what the next move was. Things had not gone according to plan and if they were to continue, they would have to discuss it. The occupant gave no additional information to the caller, and instead began humming to the music playing on the iPod...then the phone went silent.

Vhannie and Detective Peoples began dating shortly after the robbery at her branch. On the following Friday, She received a dozen roses...all pink. The card was signed 'Peoples'. Vhannie smiled, and then called to say they had brightened her day. Although the investigation into her husband's death yielded no suspects, Peoples always seem to find a reason to call. At first the phone calls were brief, and centered on the investigation. But after a month and no further leads had come in, the investigation became a cold case. Peoples still found reasons to call and/or drop by, especially around lunch time. They discovered they both had a passion for debate; Vhannie was much better read than he and her arguments more logically sound, so she usually won. If there had been a commentator to keep score, she would have been declared the winner. Regardless, the debates continued. The heat generated from the verbal confrontations intensified their love making. Peoples loved to talk during sex and in between sighs and moans he would continue arguing his point...thrusting with each verbal proclamation until they both climaxed, saying, "I think I made my point!"

After a few months of reconnecting, Vhannie discovered she was pregnant and broke the news to Peoples, expecting a joyous reception followed by hugs and kisses. What she got was a question, "Is it mine?" he asked. "What?" she responded, "Did you ask if it was yours…are you kidding? This is not the time for you to behave immaturely, are you trying to be funny?!" "No," he said, "is it mine? I can ask that if I want to. Why do you look shocked that I asked? Just because the sex is good doesn't mean the baby is mine. I don't know who visits you when I'm not around." Vhannie looked at Peoples in disbelief. She held back her tears and anger, saying only, "Yes, it is yours, but it doesn't have to be if you don't want it."

For six months, neither spoke to the other until one day when Vhannie saw Peoples at a community event where she was the guest speaker. The event was sponsored by the City's Business Chamber when she had been asked to speak about financial literacy and how to obtain a mortgage. The minority community had been plagued by unscrupulous lenders and predatory banks, causing people to become cynical and jaded and feeling that home ownership was neither affordable nor practical. Peoples had been persuaded to talk about the impact of juvenile crime and its effect on the city's crime rate. When their eyes met neither could speak, but their eyes spoke loudly and clearly. After the event was over, Peoples drove to her house.

When Vhannie heard the doorbell chime, she knew instantly it was him. She drew a deep breath and began to talk to herself, reminding herself of how he'd left her hurt and angry. She heard his words again, *'Is it mine ... just because the sex is good, that doesn't mean it's my baby'*. She wanted the memory of the hurt to protect her from the love she knew would return when she opened the door. The doorbell chimed again and she stood against the door crying silently and refusing to open it. The chime was replaced by a knock. Not loud, rather a tap…then another tap…then his voice, "Vhannie, open the door. I know you're there and I need to talk to you." She stood still against the door, crying, wondering if he could hear the sound of her heart beating. He pressed his face against the door and spoke again, "Baby, I am sorry … I am sorry and need to look at you and tell you face-to-face and feel your breath on my face … I need to look at you, and feel your eyes on me. I need to hear your voice no matter what sound it makes … I need to know that the sound is for me. Please open the door and stand before me, in judgment or forgiveness, but let me in so that I can see you and know that you see me. She opened the door and took a deep breath as he grabbed her hand. They cried together and stood there, still, cradled in each other's arms … no sound or movement except for the ticking of the clock on the wall was heard.

Peoples never verbally apologized for denying the baby and Vhannie never discussed the fact that she had miscarried 2 weeks after telling him she was pregnant. Life went on and their relationship managed itself; neither one wanting to admit that things had changed and that nothing would be the same. They went back to their routine of early week luncheons and passionate love making sessions. Vhannie never got pregnant again. The pregnancy uncovered some issues she had not been aware of. An annual physical revealed large fibroids that made her essentially sterile, unable to carry a baby to term. The doctor explained that the tumors were the reason for the miscarriage. She never shared the news with Peoples, feeling it better to let sleeping dogs lie than to bring up the hurt and shame she had felt. They enjoyed each other's company and continued their lustful debates. Kansas City continued to be the town known for barbecue, baseball, football and growing crime, especially in the inner cities.

One summer day a decapitated head was found in a trash bag in a park by a man walking with a stick. The news reported the man using the stick struck the bag and found a head belonging to an unidentified 3 year old little girl who the press renamed Precious Doe. Television and radio stations broke the news, and each day people would gather at the park where the child's head was found. Residents who had no familial relationship to the child cried as they searched the park alongside the police and local activists. Peoples, though not assigned to the case, was ever-present at any and all gatherings, looking for suspects and listening for any news that would lead to an arrest. His visit to Niece's increased as he waited for someone to make a mistake and say something that would lead to a break in the case. It so preoccupied Peoples that he and Vhannie rarely saw each other; when they did, the tension in the room was as thick as a dense fog with no visibility and no news of when it would lift. One night, after a long day of feeling he was on the wrong side of the law Peoples drove over to see her. With a bottle of cognac in his hand and a newspaper under his arm, he walked into the house.

She greeted him with a kiss on the cheek only to feel a wetness she had never felt before. When she looked into his eyes she saw why; Peoples was crying. He walked past her into the kitchen and found a glass. He put a few cubes of ice in the glass, poured cognac in and handed it to her. Then he turned the bottle up to his mouth and drank until it was empty. She looked at him and said nothing. He grabbed her hand and led her into the bedroom. He sat down on the bed, bringing her down with him, and began to take her clothes off. Vhannie allowed the silence and actions to dictate the moment. Once he had removed all of her clothes he laid her down on the bed and began to undress. He lay next to her, placing his head on her belly. Vhannie could feel the wetness from his cheeks on her stomach and lay still as he cried. Then, he was on top of her, kissing her cheeks, her eyes, her forehead and her nose … the kisses were still wet with his tears.

He began to kiss her breasts and then her belly, where he lingered for what seemed an eternity. She never moved, fearing the interruption, not knowing or understanding what was happening with her lover. He went down to her place of beginning … where life emerged and where she was different than he … and he lingered there until she felt her love for him take shape and erupt, and in the warmth surrendered her *being*. Then he was inside of her, moving to a sound and beat only he heard … feeling her tighten around him and making him manly and vulnerable. His cheeks were still wet … and then the waters rushed over him and he was swept away with the images he had brought with him. The cognac could not chase them away.

After he left, she turned on the news. Live, late breaking news on the Precious Doe case was all over the TV screen. The four-year-long mystery had been solved as Kansas City Police identified the remains of Precious Doe and charged two people in the case. Her killers turned out to be her parents. The news reported that the little girl's stepfather became enraged with the child because she'd refused to go to bed. The stepfather, under the influence of alcohol and PCP, became angry and kicked her, later throwing her to the ground causing her to hit her head and fall unconscious. She had been left on the floor for two days. Neither parent sought help for the child because both had outstanding warrants. The couple took the child's body to a church parking lot and through the woods where the father cut the child's head off with hedge clippers. The child's body was found first; then the head was discovered. The remains had been a mystery for four years until then. Vhannie fell to the couch with disbelief and sadness. She understood Peoples' tears. She looked around the house until she found the newspaper Peoples had under his arm when he arrived and read the headline: Precious Doe Identified...Murdered by Parents!

Life for Peoples underwent a metamorphosis. He continued to work each case with the same vigor and determination as before, except he began to question the purpose of relationships. He struggled to understand how a person could allow another human being to influence them in the destruction of a child. Each child abduction case became personal. Whenever a parent called or came to the precinct to report a child missing, he found himself investigating the parents with or without cause. He would do a background check on the parents to see if they were who they said they were: whether he was assigned the case or not, he sought answers. Sometimes he would drive by the parent's home and setup surveillance without the approval of the captain. He became obsessed with trying to protect children.

One night, a report came through that a young child, 10 years old, was playing in his yard when a man in a blue Ford truck attempted to lure him out of his yard and into the truck. Luckily, the child ran into his home and alerted his parents, who reported the attempted abduction to the police station. Peoples had just arrived when the report came in and without hesitation got into his car and followed the parent's home. Once in the neighborhood, he began to drive around searching for the blue Ford truck. The parents had not been able to determine the year of the truck, just that it had been a newer model and driven by a large male around thirty- to forty-years old. The suspect had long brown hair and wore a KC Royals blue baseball cap. The child was not sure if the man had a beard or mustache, but he did describe the man as having bad teeth. Peoples drove around for several hours not wanting to stop looking for the perpetrator until daylight. He went home vowing to return the next night and the next until he was comfortable that he had done a thorough search.

About a week had gone by when once again a call came through the police station saying a male in a blue Ford truck had attempted to abduct a five-year-old boy at a park. This time the mother was able to give a better description of the truck and the license plate. Peoples had his usual cup of coffee at Niece's listening for any information on the murder of Michael Groves when he returned to his car and heard the description on the radio. He went to the area of the park where the suspect had been sighted and began to look for the blue Ford truck. For four hours he searched but could not find the vehicle. Then, almost five hours into his search, he spotted it. The truck pulled up to a bar and a large man got out and went inside. Peoples parked several feet away and, after the man got out, circled the truck looking for any signs of damage or other identifying marks. The license plate was a hit for the description the mother had given. After several minutes, the man returned to his vehicle and drove away. Peoples followed him and parked across the street to observe. The man pulled into the driveway of an elegant house surrounded by trees and a well-manicured lawn. As he got out of the car and went to the front door, the porch light came on. The entire house seemed to be illuminated and inside the large man began talking to a small woman holding a child. Then Peoples saw two more children appear running and jumping on the large man. He picked up the children and began to play 'horsey', allowing the children to ride his back like a giant horse. Peoples smiled in disgust as he watched the man interact with his children. He stayed for as long as the light was on in the home. After the lights went out and he was sure the pedophile was in for the night, he drove home.

Stank met Peoples at the door and let out a low growl since he had been cooped up in the house for over ten hours without a chance to relieve himself. Peoples scratched his head and led him out into the back yard. Stank lumbered his way around until he found a spot to relieve himself. He rolled around the yard, chased a squirrel or two and then galloped his way back to the door to be allowed in. Peoples fed Stank, made a sandwich for himself and slowly began an online search to discover who the large man with the small wife and manicured lawn was, in addition to his job as a pedophile.

A SICK PERVERSION

His name was David Jacobs. He owned one of the largest construction companies in Kansas City. He was responsible for some of the most recognized buildings downtown. It was his firm who started the resurgence of downtown, bringing it back to life with loft apartment living rivaling that seen in larger metropolitan cities like Chicago and New York. He was smart, educated and had lots of money. He also had a penchant for little children, and he was going to be caught. Peoples would see to it. For the next couple of days he watched as Jacobs switched license plates and drove a different truck. The blue Ford was being transported to another town. Peoples watched as the tow truck came to the house and hauled away the evidence. He should have told the captain, but he decided he would see this one to the end. He wanted to make Jacobs pay ... and he did not want to play by the rules. Things were different now and his role as detective was becoming less important than his desire to catch the bastard. Peoples wanted to be judge and jury.

A week passed and sightings of the large man in the blue Ford truck ceased. No one except Peoples knew why. Parents of small children were taking precautions and no child was being allowed to play outside without supervision. David Jacobs came and went as he pleased. One day Peoples noticed Jacobs driving a new black Ford Explorer. He sat outside Jacobs' house each night and watched the cars come and go. The wife drove a Honda Accord with car seats and toys as so many moms do, placating rambunctious kids as she went about her daily excursions. Jacobs had several cars, but he preferred trucks, probably because of his large frame. Then he came home with the black Ford Explorer. It was newer than the blue Ford truck, but Jacobs didn't care about how new it was, his only concern was to lure young children into it. Peoples watched as he loaded one of the car seats from the Honda Accord into the Explorer. "Interesting," Peoples thought, "give the appearance of a family man with small children and no one would suspect him of hurting them." Jacobs loaded the car seat in the back and then he climbed in the driver's seat. Peoples watched as the Explorer drove down the street. It was just about dusk and the street lights had not come on yet.

After riding through several blocks, the Explorer came to a stop on a block where three small children played in a yard. There were two small boys' ages five and seven, and a little girl around four years old. He watched as the black Explorer came closer to where the children played. He watched the pedophile lower his window and noticed the blank stare on the faces of the children as they listened to the pleadings of the man in the truck. Peoples could not hear what was being said, but he could imagine the large man was asking the children to come to him. The little girl started to back away and ran toward the porch. The seven year old started to walk toward the truck when the little girl began to cry. The third child stood frozen, as the scene unfolded around him. Suddenly, the older child ran away from the truck and into the house. The black Explorer sped away and Peoples followed it.

David Jacobs was frustrated, and angry that he had been unable to lure a child into his truck. He drove through several neighborhoods before finally calling it a night. Peoples watched as he parked his truck in the driveway. Tonight he did not turn on the porch light or the light to expose the activities in the living room, instead he went into his children's room and played daddy. Peoples sat in his car, contemplating what he should tell his captain or the rest of the police force about David Jacobs. Only problem was he had not found out anything. Sure, he could have told them about the blue Ford truck being transported to God-knows-where, but what he really needed was hard evidence, and he had none. There would be no way the captain would have brought David Jacobs in for questioning considering how many important people he knew. Peoples knew he needed to get something real on Jacobs, like catching him luring a child into his truck, and arrest him on the spot. He was anxious about catching the pervert, except he didn't have anything on him, not just yet. Peoples knew it was a matter of time before Jacobs slipped, and when he did, he would be there to catch him.

Jacobs changed cars again. The same tow truck pulled up to the house and loaded the black Explorer on the bed, and once it was secured the truck was gone. Peoples sat across the street and watched Jacobs come out of the house and get into his wife's Honda. He followed the Accord to a local Ford dealership. Jacobs went inside and onto the sales floor. Minutes later he was getting into a white Ford truck. The white truck trailed the Honda back to Jacobs' residence. Peoples smiled as a familiar tingle came over him. Tonight, he felt, would be the night David Jacobs would slip up.

Vhannie saw less and less of Peoples as he chased the pedophile. She knew nothing about his plan to catch Jacobs, or any other case he was investigating. She only knew he had little time for her, and she was feeling neglected. She called and left messages that were never returned. She went by his house a few times and knocked on the door, but when she heard Stank's growl she knew he wasn't home. She didn't know who to contact, because he never introduced her to his family. She felt lost, confused and lonely; she didn't know what to think. So as any woman in love would do, she began to imagine he was seeing someone else, someone younger and prettier with a big butt and bigger boobs, who didn't have a lot of brains, but made him feel like a big Stud. She tried to remember a time when maybe he had introduced her to someone, or had spoken the name of a woman she'd never met, but no one came to mind. That did not stop her mind from wandering. So she waited for him to call so she could confront him.

Peoples went on about the business of catching his pedophile. He continued to observe Jacobs' comings and goings. Mornings, afternoons and nights he watched … and waited for the right time. Nothing happened. It was as if Jacobs knew something. Peoples became restless and thought maybe he had lost his taste for little kids. One day while at the station, he overheard some people talk about an event downtown that included several big names around town. The event included an awards banquet and benefit auction, and Jacobs would be there. Peoples prepared to stake out the event. He would watch David Jacobs, he might even approach him. He had that old detective feeling in his balls. They began to twitch and he knew the sign, he was going to catch him. Tonight he would do something, something that would be his undoing. So Peoples went home to get ready.

The doorbell rang as Stank made his way to the door. Peoples was in the shower and had not heard the first ring. The doorbell rang again, this time he heard it. Wrapping a towel around his waist he went to the door. Just as he began to ask who it was, he heard the sound of glass breaking. He hurried toward a window which offered him a view of his drive way. He saw nothing so he let Stank out. He went back to the bathroom to begin shaving when he heard Stank make a noise he knew all too well. It was the sound he made when Vhannie was around. Then he heard a knock at the door. As he opened the door, Vhannie looked at him as if she wanted to slap him. Peoples smiled and attempted to hug her as she stepped inside. She looked around as if he was hiding someone and she was determined to find her. She headed toward the living room, with Stank close by her side pushing her hand along his back as he growled. She stroked him as he slowly rolled over on his back so that she could scratch his tummy. "Hello," said Peoples, "I know we haven't been seeing much of each other, but baby I have been really busy. What about you, haven't you been busy too?" "“Lang what is going on with you? It has been over three weeks and you haven't had a minute available for phone call or text … really? Look, if you are that busy then what are you getting dressed for? A date?"

She walked into the living room and sat on the sofa. Peoples was nervous as he wondered how he was going to get her out of the house so he could get dressed. He needed to get to the convention center where the banquet was being held and she was preventing him from getting ready. He walked back into the bathroom and yelled out the door, "Baby, go ahead and make us a couple of drinks." Peoples had to think fast, first he'd kiss her a little, then he'd tell her how much he missed her and then just when the alcohol began to send warmth thru her body his phone would ring. Yeah, he thought that's what I'll do. He knew his smart phone would come in handy one day. Normally Peoples hated his phone, and only answered it for her and his mother. But since Vhannie was already there and his mother was away in Greece he would have to figure something else out. He would pretend it was the job calling about a case, a call he had to take. Lucky for him the little cute blonde girl at the cell phone kiosk showed him how to make his phone call his own number.

Yeah he thought, I'll tell her to relax and stay the night and as soon as I'm done, I'll come back and take care of her. He knew what she really came over for, it was for some loving. It had been a while since the two of them had made love and if it hadn't been for the disgusting pedophile in their midst, he would have both her legs around his back! He knew what she needed and he was the only man for her. Making love to Vhannie was better than any woman he had ever been with. She was so passionate and expressive. Peoples loved the way she moaned and groaned and how she gave instructions demanding he go deeper and deeper. When she climaxed she sang a little song under her breath. He knew he was the only man who made her sing and it had been a long time since she'd sang.

He walked into the living room and noticed Stank had managed to get on the sofa and onto her lap. Vhannie sipped her drink and looked at Peoples with sadness on her face. "Look," she said, "I didn't mean to interrupt you, but you seem to be preoccupied with something or someone and if it's another woman, then just say so." Peoples went to the sofa and pushed Stank to the floor, and then he laid his head in her lap. "Baby, I know it's been a long time since we've been together. It's the job. You know I'm still working the Michael's case and now they're talking about gangs on the south east side. I miss us too." Peoples stood, bringing her to her feet at the same time. He pulled her close and began kissing her neck. He knew that was her trigger. He slowly kissed her neck and began to softly suck as he kissed. Her breathing began to quicken and her hands tightened around his back. She arched her back to get closer to him and started to feel for the bulge in his pants when his cell phone rang. Peoples moved away from her and went to the bathroom to answer his phone. When he came out he was fully dressed and said he had to leave. "Stay baby, I'll be back just got a call to go and assist on the eastside. Gangs," he said and then left.

The convention center was buzzing with important men standing around debating politics and women commenting on clothes and hair. The gowns were expensive and tight-fitting. The tuxedos were rented and the buttons were strained. Music was blasting … Stevie Wonder one minute and Hank Williams the next. The servers wore white shirts, black slacks and red cummerbunds. The bar was open and whiskey flowed. David Jacobs arrived with his petite wife. They were immediately greeted by the mayor and his wife. David's wife, Élan, a red-head with green eyes was smart, funny, and eager to please any and every one she met. Standing next to Jacobs she presented an interesting sight. Most people would respond, "Is that your daughter?" Jacobs never found it especially amusing since she was 20 years his junior. They had been married for ten years.

She had worked for him as an intern during the demolition of a large apartment building. Élan had been an excellent student and very bright. The office manager often partnered with the local community colleges looking for interns to coach and train while they completed their college degrees. She had been looking for extra money and a chance to get into the construction business, so when her instructor told her about the job, she jumped at it. Each day, Jacobs would come in and comment on her hair or something she wore. He liked to tell her how pretty she was and how smart women were often overlooked. He, on the other hand, loved smart women, especially red-heads. He bought her lunch or would take her out. Soon she was seen less and less in the office and more and more on the job site talking to him and looking pretty.

Six months into her new career he asked her out on a date, and she agreed. The date was normal, dinner and a movie. When he took her home, he asked if he could come in. She said yes and two hours later she was being smothered by his enormous body. Élan realized she had better make him stay. She wanted to be married and she knew he was a good catch, even if he was awkward in bed, too big and too rough to please her. She knew he knew how to make money, so she faked the first orgasm and every one after that. After about a dozen or so he proposed, and she accepted. Two years into the marriage, she gave birth to a little boy, three years after, a girl. Later, after all the faking and the birth of her children, he no longer prompted her for sex. Instead he spent hours on his computer, or driving around at night, which he said relaxed him. She was relieved.

The crowd grew larger and so did the laughter. Someone hired a comedian, and the jokes were becoming raunchier as the drinks got stronger. A glass fell on the floor as a pretty lady began reaching for napkins to dab away the spill. Peoples walked in and was greeted by a very effeminate young man who offered to get him anything he wanted. Peoples refused the drinks and the 'anything' offered by the young man as he headed toward the front of the room. He stopped as he got close to his suspect. Jacobs was laughing and drinking and never noticed the man who would change his life.

The speaker made his way to the stage and began talking about how great Kansas City was and all the industry coming to the area. There was a hush in the crowd and someone yelled "Google!" The speaker seized the moment to introduce the mayor. The crowd erupted with cheers and glasses rose in the air. The mayor began by praising the CEO's of the area and recognizing all the great men and women who were there to see Kansas City become the greatest city west of the Mississippi. "Yes," he said, "we are getting Google fiber and it will change the way KC does business. Neighborhoods will increase in value as Google fiber is installed throughout the metro area. We are the first city to have this remarkable service and it will revolutionize the way we watch TV, run our computers and use our phones." "This, the mayor said, "is just the beginning of a wonderful affair." The crowd cheered again and side conversations could be overheard as the mayor continued to speak. Peoples looked around the room taking in all sights, sounds and objects. He needed to be aware of his surroundings. Most people he knew never paid attention to small details, missing things that gave the upper hand to the criminal, and he knew of at least one criminal in the room.

Jacobs was seated on a big chair in a corner of the room, his wife at his side, laughing each time he made a joke. There were at least two other couples around the Jacobs, drinking wine and encouraging his sad comedic routine. A small man with a gray jacket and blue slacks yelled across the room at Jacobs, indicating some familiarity. Jacobs got up and headed in the man's direction. His pretty red-headed wife stayed put. She looked as though someone had unplugged the music. Jacobs walked up to the man and put his hand on the man's shoulder. The man started talking, but Jacobs seemed uninterested. After about twenty minutes, the man walked away like a wounded puppy with its tail between its legs. Jacobs started laughing as he made his way to the bar. He downed one drink and walked back to his seat with another in hand. Peoples watched as the big man got more drunk, and drunker still. The waiters and waitresses encouraged everyone to be seated as they began serving dinner. Élan thought, "Not a minute too soon." She knew her husband would drink too much; he always did at social gatherings. She knew he'd end up in a heated discussion about illegal immigration and eventually be asked to leave. But he was one of the biggest developers around town, and everyone wanted to be his friend. Most just wanted to work with him, but nothing else.

No one had a good impression about him; to the contrary, most of his colleagues thought he was peculiar. Élan's parents hated him and secretly wished one day he would get seriously hurt or die at one of the work sites. They were grateful for the standard of living he provided for Élan and the children, but felt he was not a very nice person. Everyone knew he was smart and hardworking, but he was also a bully and if he knew something about you he could use as leverage, he would. He had one brother who lived in Detroit. There were no nieces or nephews and his parents were killed in a house fire when David was twenty and away at college.

So he became the master of his own destiny. His first job was with an old Jewish guy who thought David was just the right person to groom and mentor. He took a liking to him the first time they met. David, fresh out of college with a degree in construction design, walked into the office and asked for the owner of the business. The receptionist asked him who he was and if he had an appointment. David said no, "But he knows me and he'll be excited to see me again." The receptionist went into the office of her boss and said "David Jacobs is here to see you." After that meeting they became inseparable and David Jacobs became one of the top business developers in Kansas City.

Peoples went outside to the parking garage and looked for the white truck he knew Jacobs drove. It was nowhere to be found. Most of KC that night drove Mercedes', Lincolns, Cadillacs, Lexus' and Infinity's. He wondered if the Jacobs drove themselves or if they rode with one of the couples he'd seen them talking to. Just as he was about to go in, he saw the small man in the gray jacket and decided to follow him. The man walked quickly toward a van with cheap wheels. Peoples thought the car looked out of place and wondered who it belonged to. As the man approached, Peoples noticed a piece of paper in his hand. The man walked to the driver's side of the van and placed the paper underneath the front tire wheel. Then he watched the man go in the opposite direction, enter a blue Ford Taurus, and drive away.

Peoples was intrigued and excited at the same time. Not only did David Jacobs like to pick up little kids but apparently he had issues with small men who liked to place notes indiscriminately. He had to think quickly: should he retrieve the paper, read it and place it back under the wheel, or should he wait for the owner of the van to arrive and see if it belonged to Jacobs? Either way, he knew he would follow that note and he was sure it would lead him to Jacobs. So he waited for the party to end.

Vhannie and Stank lay down across the king-sized bed in Peoples bedroom. Stank stretched his large, stocky body across Vhannie's legs, but after a few minutes they started to lose circulation. As she pushed against him, he turned his head toward her as if to say she was disturbing his rest. She turned the TV on and began watching an old Clint Eastwood movie. She didn't like Westerns, but liked Clint. Peoples liked all Westerns, especially John Wayne films. Whenever he planned date night for them, it always included a John Wayne Western and a bottle of whiskey. John Wayne with swag … that's how Peoples liked to think of himself. So when it was Vhannie's turn to plan date night, she rented horror movies and made him bring the whiskey. Neither one liked it when it was the others turn. The movie was a good one though, *Pale Rider*. She went into the kitchen, popped a bag of popcorn, added a little red pepper and got a bottle of beer. As she started to settle into the softness of the comforter, the doorbell rang. She thought it was strange since she had never known Peoples to receive company. He hated for people to stop by without calling. But even if they called, he wouldn't answer and then he wouldn't answer the door either. So this was unusual and no one knew she was there. She hesitated, and then decided she would wait to see if they would go away. Stank was already at the door, growling. He never barked, always a low guttural growl indicating that to enter would clearly mean trouble. The doorbell rang again followed by a knock. Vhannie got closer to the door, pointing at Stank not to move. Then the sound of an engine replaced the knock. The uninvited guest had left.

The ceremony at the convention center was ending and Peoples had found the perfect waiting spot. From his vantage point he could see everyone. One by one they exited into the parking garage. Engines roared as dignitaries played follow-the-leader back to their suburban homes. Peoples smiled, amused at the idea that so many who made decisions about the city didn't really live in the city. They lived as far away as was politically correct to protect their jobs. He waited for what felt like an hour, and finally he saw them; the large pedophile and the red-headed accommodating wife. They walked to a Honda Accord. "What," Peoples thought, "they actually drove her car?" He was surprised, but not disappointed; he just needed to adjust his plan. He decided to follow them anyway. He thought about hanging around to see who drove the van with the note in the wheel, but that wasn't what he was there for. No, he was there for Jacobs and he'd find out who the small man was later if he needed to know.

He followed them as they drove down I-435 headed west. Once they arrived at the house, he backed off and parked several houses down. He knew they hadn't seen him. Peoples was a very good detective and he knew how to follow without being noticed. He was a top cop, who was determined to arrest Jacobs. The lights in the house came on, and the scene he witnessed shocked him to the core. He had to blink his eyes twice, trying to refocus, not believing what he was seeing. Right in front of him, he watched as Élan punched her husband in the gut. Peoples shook his head in disbelief not at the punch, but at Jacobs' reaction. He looked as if he were really hurt. He fell forward and landed on the sofa. Then Élan walked over to him and started punching him in the face. He threw his hands up for protection, but she continued. Blow after blow, she seemed to gain strength unknown to such a small woman, and continued to strike him wherever she saw an opening. Peoples could tell both were speaking, but he couldn't make out what was being said. He knew the words were not sweet and loving, they were probably, "Stop, please stop." He hesitated for just a moment, contemplating whether or not to call in the domestic fight, but then he knew he couldn't. He could care less that Jacobs was getting his butt whipped. He continued to look and actually started to enjoy the fight scene. They continued for about thirty minutes, Élan throwing blows and Jacobs receiving them. It was like watching an underweight against a heavy weight. This, Peoples thought, was too good to be true. Just as quickly as they started, the attack ended. He could see Élan leave the living room and Jacobs lying curled on the sofa like a big old fat cat. Peoples waited for another thirty minutes expecting Jacobs to get into his truck and go hunting for small, innocent children. He never did that night. He simply retreated to his bedroom after turning off the living room lights.

Peoples drove home replaying the events that unfolded before him. He tried to connect the dots: Jacobs goes to an event with his wife, is approached by a small man in a gray jacket who puts a piece of paper underneath the car of someone who isn't Jacobs; Peoples follows Jacobs and his wife home and witnesses a domestic offense committed by the wife. If he hadn't seen it, he wouldn't have believed it. Strange, he thought, but it would not stop him from pursuing Jacobs and arresting him before he molested another child. As he drove into his garage he remembered Vhannie was still there.

He had forgotten about her unexpected visit and that things between them had not been good lately. He wondered what he would encounter when he entered the house. He opened the door and

Stank did not greet him, instead he just raised his big head up and looked at him. He was so comfortable on the bed with Vhannie that he didn't want to leave. Peoples smiled as he looked at the beauty and the beast lying on his bed. He tried not to wake her as he went into the bathroom and prepared for bed. He checked his underarms and his breath just to be sure everything was still fresh. He had only been gone a few hours and hadn't had to chase anyone so he didn't think he needed a shower. He splashed on a little cologne just in case she woke and wanted to make love. He felt up to it, after all it had been a while and making love to Vhannie was always good. One good orgasm and he would be out like a light! When he got to the bed she was still asleep with all her clothes were on. He touched her face and spoke softly in her ear. "Baby, I'm home. Let's get you out of those clothes." He was kissing her face and then her neck. She opened her eyes and grabbed him close to her, crying into his chest. "Baby, what's wrong?" he said, "I'm here, and everything is okay." Stank lumbered out of the bed and into his room, hating to leave the big bed, but knowing it was time to leave the two of them alone. She started to speak but the tears were making it impossible to understand. So Peoples held her and rocked her in his arms. She looked up at him with wet eyes and said, "I missed you so much. I thought you didn't want to be together anymore, you haven't been around, no calls, no visits, nothing."

"Is it someone else Peoples, is that it, have you found someone else?" He looked surprised and started to laugh, but sensing how emotional she was at that moment, the smarter side of him took over. He shook his head, and kissed her. He took her hand in his and kissed it. Then he started to remove her blouse. She lay back and put her hands around his neck. He took off her skirt and then her panties. She looked directly in his eyes trying to see inside of him. He felt her stare but continued to undress her until she was completely naked. Then he moved her hands from around his neck and began taking off his shorts. She looked at him again trying to capture his gaze, but instead he lay on top of her and began kissing her eyes. She wrapped her arms around him and started kissing his neck and shoulders. He kissed her long and deep. Stopping between kisses to tell her how much he missed her. He kissed her breast, licking each nipple and gently pausing for the right sound. He knew the sounds she made when he aroused her. They made him hard. She started to moan and sigh….that was it; that was what he was waiting for. She arched her back off the bed at the erotic feeling coursing through her body. He sucked longer and his mouth became very wet, so wet the saliva dripped off her onto the bed. She moaned louder and started begging him to enter her. He continued to kiss as he went down and inside her thighs licking and licking her until she grabbed the bed and begged again for him to be inside of her. Then he positioned himself to go inside her. She moaned as she wrapped her strong legs around his back. He looked deep into her eyes as if trying to read her mind. And with each stroke, he told her there was no one else for him. He continued reassuring her and looking deeper into her eyes. She looked at him and held him tighter. Kissing his face, shoulders, chest, eyes, and then his mouth, she told him that she loved him too. They fell asleep.

The next morning, she got out of the bed and looked back at the man she loved more and more each day, wondering if he felt the same. Stank was awake too and walked up to her hand moving it with his big head. This was his way of letting her know he had to go outside. Stank was a good dog, no bad habits she could think of and he liked her. She remembered when Peoples mentioned he was going to get a dog. She didn't think it was such a good idea since he wasn't home a lot, but it had worked out. Stank and Peoples had grown together. Stank had gotten use to Peoples being away and having the house to himself. He never made mistakes in the house. It was amazing to her how long he could control himself and not potty in the house. Peoples grew accustomed to Stank's low growl and his inability to learn tricks. Maybe, Peoples thought, he just doesn't like tricks; he was a very independent dog, just like his master.

The sound and smell of bacon frying and coffee brewing got Peoples out of bed and in the kitchen. He wrapped his arms around Vhannie and kissed her on the cheek. "Good morning beautiful." She turned toward him and returned the favor. He grabbed his favorite coffee mug and began to pour a cup adding a little sweetener. No cream for him, he liked his coffee strong and black ... just like her he'd say with a big grin on his face. She poured herself some and turned on the small television. The news was on and the anchor was reporting in front of the convention hall recapping the night's events. Camera shots of women and men all dressed up entering the center was plastered all over the set. Then a close up of the mayor with David Jacobs interrupted Peoples thoughts. He began to feel the anger again as he watched the pervert cohort with the Mayor and other city officials. Vhannie didn't pay any attention to Peoples, instead she began preparing Stank's food. He sat at the island in his kitchen, then got up and went into his office and closed the door. He started looking through a folder he kept locked in his desk drawer. In it were pictures of Jacobs driving through the neighborhood, changing cars, and paying the tow truck driver to take away the black Explorer. He had also started a journal of

Jacobs' whereabouts. It was a thick folder, about thirty pages at last count. He sat and looked at the pages, not reading, just thinking that somehow he needed to get the son of a bitch degenerate. Last night was interesting, he thought, Élan beating up big old Jacobs and he cowering like a wimp. It just didn't make sense. Neither did the little man in the gray jacket. Nothing was connecting and he needed to hurry and close this case, especially since he had been working a case no one else knew existed.

Vhannie knew that whenever he went into his office, it was his time. She wouldn't disturb him, instead she found Stank's leash and prepared to go for a walk. Both dog and woman needed some get away time as well. She grabbed her cell phone and the keys to the house and closed the door behind her. Peoples never heard them leave; instead he began looking through his phone for the number of one of his informants. He knew it was long shot trying to find out who the little man was and his connection to Jacobs, but it was worth it. His guy was good at knowing everything that meant anything in the city. Even though the night's events happened in the better part of town, he might be able to help Peoples, so he dialed.

Vhannie and Stank had gotten through the neighborhood and was headed to the wooded area behind the house. She never really liked to walk through the area, usually Peoples walked with her so she felt safe, but today it was just her and Stank. He loved exploring the woods, so Peoples was happy the house included the rural area, dog and trees were a match made in heaven. Off they went, into the woods. Stank performed well when he went for walks, never pulling the leash and always staying at her side, so when he yanked her and lunged at something behind a bush, she almost panicked. He was so strong, that she lost her footing and fell down on one knee cell phone flying the opposite direction. The leash fell out of her hand and Stank ran toward the thing in the woods. She looked around her for the cell phone, yelling his name at the same time. "Stank!" she yelled. "Stank, come here!" She got up and started in the direction he had run, obviously sensing a threat. Stank was not the type of dog that ran after every squirrel, cat or dog he saw; he was a trained guard dog. He never lashed out at people; instead he watched and waited for any moment to indicate his master was being attacked. Then Stank would become a formidable weapon. Vhannie yelled his name and looked for him through the tall trees. Finally, he emerged with a piece of fabric in his teeth. She took it from his mouth. He sat down next to her, waiting for her to reattach the leash. She was puzzled at his reaction and at the sight of the material in his mouth.

As she secured the leash, she realized the fabric was the type typically used to make men's pants. She began to worry, and became anxious as she called Peoples' cell. He didn't answer. Her anxiety rose at his failure to pick up. She called again … again no answer. She grabbed Stank's leash and began to run through the woods, the dog running at her side, until they got to the clearing where she could again see the house... As she approached, she saw a car backing out of the driveway. She grabbed her phone and began calling Peoples again. Stank ran ahead of her, aimed for the car. The driver saw them coming and peeled out of the driveway, barely missing Stank's hind legs. The front door opened and Peoples ran toward them. Looking confused and angry, he watched the car drive away. He had a strange feeling as he walked the pair back into the house: the car was the same one he'd seen the little man drive away in at the convention center. Vhannie wrapped her arms around Peoples as she began to describe the events that unfolded earlier. "Stank has never run away from me, he always obeys the walking rules, but he spotted someone or something in the woods behind the house and ran after it. He is so strong that when he lurched, I fell down. When I got up and called for him, he came back to me with a piece of cloth in his mouth. I tried to call you; I must have called three or four times, but you wouldn't answer. I was so scared, I didn't know what was happening." "Okay babe," he answered, engulfing her in his strong arms, "everything is okay now. Stank will always protect you and you know that, right? Right? I'm sorry I didn't answer the phone; I was reading a report and got carried away. Do you think you recognized the person in the car? Do you think it could have been the person in the woods?" "I don't know," she said, "I didn't get a look at him, all I got was this piece of cloth that Stank tore from him." Vhannie's tone was high-pitched, her breathing fast as she continued to rant about how frightened she'd become. Peoples looked at Stank as the dog went to his bed, and curled up for a nap, completely unbothered by the event.

His phone buzzed. Peoples glanced down as a text message appeared from his informant, saying he thought he knew who the small man was and that he could meet him somewhere to give him the information. Peoples put his phone into his pocket, and sat next to Vhannie on the sofa. Her arms were folded across her chest, and she looked very worried. He remembered the same worry on her face earlier when he told her they had found Michael's body in the motel. He knew Vhannie was strong and resilient, but today's events had shaken her to the core and seeing her like that, he felt the need to protect her. He wanted to call his informant, but knew he couldn't leave her, not even for a minute. He went into the kitchen, fixed them both a drink, and sat next to her again on the sofa. They talked about everything except what had just happened; he needed to get her mind off it.

He got up, gathered his music collection and began to play some old-school R&B. He knew just the thing to get her into a different mood. First he played Jill Scott, then Eric Benet, and finally some Teddy P! Teddy Pendergrass always put her in a playful mood and tonight was no exception. Vhannie started to relax and even Stank got into the act. He stretched out on the floor by her feet waiting for her to remove her shoes and rub her feet up and down his tummy. Peoples smiled as he watched both his best friends relax. The day was almost over, night had begun to fall. He looked through his music collection and pulled out a blues CD: Bobby Womack, *Wish You Didn't Trust Me So Much*. Peoples loved that song, even though it was about a two-timing friend having the hots for another man's woman. Tonight, it was about Jacobs. He would get close to Jacobs, so close that he would think Peoples was his best friend … and then he'd get him.

THE SMALL MAN

The small man drove home and took off his torn pants. He was not aware of the dog as he waited in the woods behind People's house. He had been told about the previous break-in and knew Peoples had a gun, but not a big dog who'd try to tear a hole into him. He threw the ripped pants into a bag along with the shirt he wore. He sweated so bad that the shirt was stained beyond cleaning. He was taking a shower when he heard the doorbell. Because he knew who was on the other side he hesitated to answer it; he didn't feel like a confrontation. The visitor insisted, ringing again followed by a hard knock on the door. The small man grabbed a towel and wrapped it around his waist. He went to the door and leaned his face against the peep hole. A loud pop followed by a burst of light was all he would ever know. He fell back against the door and then crumpled to the floor.

Vhannie and Peoples went to bed, and were sound asleep when his phone rang. He thought it was his CI calling again and was irritated at the interruption. He answered, "Yeah?" but the voice on the other end was his partner. "Peoples, get your ass up, we got a dead body on the south side." Peoples sat up and gathered his wits along with his pants. "Where exactly?" he asked. His partner gave him the address and began to describe the victim, "Black male, 40-50 years old, 5'3 to 5'5 inches tall, shot in the head … Peoples, this is messed up, you need to get here, quick!" He didn't bother to shower, just grabbed a shirt and holstered his weapon. Vhannie sat up, telling him to be careful. He ran out the door and drove to the crime scene. When he arrived the area had been taped off, uniform cops were milling around, preventing nosy neighbors from contaminating the scene. His partner was inside the house along with CSI, taking pictures and collecting evidence. Peoples looked at the dead man on the floor and quickly scanned the area around him looking for clues. One spent shell casing was found next to the body. The victim had been shot at close range. The bullet had exited and lodged in the wall behind him. The man's face was a mess, barely recognizable. The white towel he had wrapped himself in was still around his small frame, turned red with his blood. He was not wearing shoes, and it appeared he had not gotten in the shower but was preparing to.

Peoples went into the next room, being careful to not disturb any evidence as he looked around for clues to the man's identity. There were only a few pictures. He noticed a trash can with clothes in it and retrieved them: a shirt and a pair of pants with a hole in them ... was this the man who had just been at his house? Surely it was not the man who Stank had torn a hole in, and who Peoples witnessed backing out of his driveway. He thought about the night at the convention center. Was this the man who approached Jacobs and then put the piece of paper in the car's wheel? Peoples began to look more intensely as thoughts raced through his mind about who this man was and what the connection between him and Jacobs was. His partner followed him into the next room and began talking about what he thought had lead up to the victims murder.

Peoples was lost in his own thoughts; how this man died was not one of them. The sound of his partner's voice became a distant murmur as he noticed a picture. A picture of a family, but the background was unusual. There was a mother, a father and 2 children 1 boy and one little girl, Peoples gathered it and placed it with the other items. There was little else in the house; half-eaten food discarded in the trash was collected by the forensic team. The rest of the victim's clothes were gathered and placed in evidence bags, along with anything else the detectives thought pertinent to the case. They went outside to look at the victim's car. It was a compact, just like the victim, simple and basic. The car was a 2005 Ford Taurus with standard equipment. No whistles or bells, not even a navigation system. The radio was basic with a single cd changer. Peoples looked around for something that made the car personal to the victim. He looked through the glove compartment hoping to find the registration papers, but no luck. He looked under seats, at the roof, in the console and then he went outside and began looking around the wheels. He noticed dirt on the tires and knew once the forensic team started to collect evidence they would match the soil to the area around his house. He hoped the dirt in the woods by his house was common dirt and no connection to him would be made. It wasn't as if he knew anything about the victim, he was attempting to find out who the small man was when all hell broke loose. Now he would have to work fast to figure out not only who the man was, but why the man had been in his driveway.

He gathered the picture and clothes he'd gotten from the house and placed them in his car. He didn't want them checked in at the station, because once they had been logged he'd have to sign them out and he didn't want any delays in trying to figure out who the man was. He wanted to conduct his own investigation into who this man was, and allowing forensics to take them would delay any chance he had at trying to figure out how he connected to this man and how the small man connected to Jacobs. He knew he was going against policy, better yet it could cost him his job, but right now he needed to figure things out before they got cold. The uniform cops stood outside as the coroner took the body to the morgue.

Peoples got into his car as his phone buzzed; it was his informant. The text said he needed Peoples to call him right away. He drove through traffic until he reached the Nickel, an area of town where his informant often hung out and that was known for drug activity. It ran north and south from 50th to 55th street. It wasn't the worst part of town, but if you didn't have to live there you wouldn't … unless it provided you with a good income. Peoples found a place to park and looked for his guy. He didn't text back, he hated that type of communication and although everyone texted these days, he was still holding out. Finally, a red motorcycle pulled up alongside his car. The CI got off the bike, walked around to the passenger side of Peoples' car, got in and immediately started talking, "Okay this dude is some type of foreigner, not sure where he's from … Africa or somewhere like Jamaica or something like that. He did work on houses around town, odds and ends working with anyone who gave him a job. From what I understand he was pretty good with cutting concrete and anything else he needed to do to make money. He was a lone ranger didn't like to take orders from anyone, hard to deal with; small man with a big attitude and a long memory. Sound like that's what got him popped." Peoples wanted to look surprised, but he knew better; anything that happened in town concerning a murder was only a 'whodunit' to the cops, the streets kept no secrets. So he didn't interrupt and listened to the description of his victim. The informant said he didn't know who did it yet, just that he knew the dude had gotten popped. "Man, I tell you what, this dude didn't really hang out much, but if I was you, I'd check with some of them cats that hang out in the Bottoms or in the north east where all the foreigners are. Better yet, you check around to a couple a' them construction sites and you're probably going to meet somebody that can tell you what time of day he got up and what time he went to bed. But if I was you, I wouldn't take a bunch of money with me; you just might get hurt and have to call the police! Ha ha!" he laughed, as he exited the car. Peoples drove away thinking about the day's events and then realized he missed Vhannie and needed to hear her voice.

She was at home when the phone rang. "Hello?" she said. Peoples asked if she was okay and why she hadn't stayed at his place. "Look babe, I know how serious things get when you have a case and I didn't think it was a good idea to stay there. I know you Lang, in between reading reports and calling witnesses, I might get one call or a text. This is what you do and I know how important your job is to you. Better yet, I know how important you are to the job. So I just made sure Stank was okay and drove home. I'm okay and everything is fine. I just called Ms. Flowers and she said the neighborhood was pretty quiet. But I do have one question for you honey," "Yes," he said, "what is it?" "Have you gotten any word yet on Michael's murder or the cause of his death?" Peoples took a deep breath, making sure she didn't hear him exhale, "Yes and no, the ME said it was due to heart failure, and that Michael had a history of heart disease, but I am sure you already knew that. So right now his case has been put on hold. I'm not sure where it will end up, but you can rest assured I'll continue to dig deep until something comes up." She smiled at the phone knowing Peoples would do just what he said he'd do. "Sounds good babe, I'm getting ready for bed and we'll talk in the morning, love you." Peoples went to the station and started working up the small man's murder.

VHANNIE AND MICHAEL

Vhannie and Michael Groves married in 2002 with little fanfare. Everyone who knew the Groves where upset when they announced they would not have a large formal wedding. They were well known throughout the city, especially the elder Groves. Everyone knew about the feud between Huber and Groves, and how Huber had killed himself in the parking lot of the church after it was discovered his wife-to-be had been born a man. Most had taken sides: people who liked Huber, hated Groves, and vice-versa. Some even thought Huber was still alive; the body found in the car with a gunshot wound had been burned beyond recognition and some people said they had seen Huber around. Others said he had moved away and ran a big church in the south. Groves, however was very much dead. Most of the city had turned out for his funeral. People from all over came to wish him farewell. Some came to be sure he was dead; they hated him and had never forgiven him for all the corruption he caused. Each pastor after him seemed to be more corrupt than the last. Greed seemed to be the only quality necessary for the pastor of Greener Pastures. But most of the city liked Michael Groves. He was as popular as his dad was unpopular. He was a jock and a gentleman. He had a very easy spirit and a huge heart. He could be seen delivering large boxes of food and clothing to the men at the city Union Mission during Thanksgiving, and he liked to prepare the turkey. He was nice and kind, although if you caught him at the wrong time, you'd see a glimmer of his dad. He could be vindictive and cunning if necessary. He knew he harbored some of his dad's undesirable traits, so he worked hard to prevent them from ever coming out. It was his kind spirit and his competitive nature that caught Vhannie's attention when they were away at college.

He was a good football player and could have gone pro, but he wanted to be like his dad; at least the good part of his dad. He wanted to be a pastor, so he never entertained the idea of playing professional football. He studied hard and earned a Bachelor's and a Master's degree in psychology. Later, he went to seminary and graduated with a degree in Divinity. Michael was the apple of his dad's eye, never giving him any problems. He studied his dad's every move. It was evident whenever he spoke at the church, whether it was leading a song or preaching a sermon, the similarities between him and his dad were remarkable. But just as they were alike, they were extremely different. The elder Groves was bitter and angry even though Huber had died and he had gotten the church, he remained a man never to cross. He made the right connections in the city and some people thought he would become city councilman, but the elder Groves had no use for politics. His only dream was to pastor his own church. He was a good pastor at times, helping to establish a food bank which was one of the largest in the city, at other times speaking at engagements to endorse a particular candidate, who for reasons others could not understand, always seem to win.

The elder Groves was known around town and not necessarily for preaching the gospel. The rumor of sleeping with other women was common of the more popular preachers, especially those that were handsome and well endowed. Both Groves had been blessed in that area, or cursed, depending on who you spoke with. Women love powerful men and the elder Groves loved women who loved him. Several times he had been found in compromising positions with female members of his congregation, and not always after church hours. On one particular occasion the choir director, a very young woman with an equally bad reputation, was caught with her dress up, bent over the pastor's desk in his office. Choir practice had been over for just 30 minutes, when the drummer knocked on the pastor's study. The two were caught up in the moment and making noises so loud, the drummer thought he needed to investigate the strange sounds. As he opened the door, he began to apologize, "S-sorry, p-pastor, I didn't know you had s-someone in here with you." The elder Groves pulled up his pants as the choir director lowered her dress. The drummer remained in the office, frozen in his tracks and afraid to say anything else. After what seemed like an eternity, the elder Groves turned to the young man and told him to sit down.

The pretty choir director walked slowly from the study looking directly at the young drummer, smiling as she passed him. "Now young man what is it that you need to see me for?" Groves sat staring at the young man as he awaited his reply. "S-S-Sir," the drummer was known to stutter whenever he was stressed or felt frightened. "I was just t-t-t-trying to see if-f-f you wanted me to go and s-s-s-start your c-c-car for you." Groves smiled and said, "You always take care of me, don't you Leroy? You are a good and kind young man, never getting involved with petty gossip and idle chatter, no not you Leroy. You are a smart kid, waiting and studying to become a man of God like me. You know Leroy, as you get older you will be able to overcome your stutter, you'll find something or someone to help you conquer that. That's what I do. Whenever I feel pressured or stressed, I relax, and sometimes the way I relax is with someone. Yeah, that young woman you saw, she helps me relax, and you know what I mean Leroy? That's what women do, they help you relax, they help you unwind and that helps you focus on God and doing his will. It is a hard thing to do; writing sermons, helping the poor, dealing with city people, trying to raise a family … these things take a toll on a man, and women, especially young women, help you through that. You'll see Leroy; it's like taking a sedative so you can sleep. You wait and see, or maybe you already know what I mean. You got a girl Leroy? What does she look like? I bet she's pretty and fine, just like that one that left my office. I bet you got more than one, don't you Leroy? Yeah, you got more than one, and I bet you make sure they don't know about each other don't you? You know that's the way you got to do that, 'cause women get their feelings hurt too easy. Always comparing themselves to each other, they don't understand why you need more than one, but you and me, we understand don't we Leroy? Yeah, you ever heard the old saying, 'never let your right hand know what your left hand is doing"? Well, that's what you and I do, we keep things quiet. There ain't no need in letting anyone, especially your woman, know about another woman. It causes problems and hurt their feelings. I don't ever want to hurt my wife's feelings and I know you keep your women protected as well." Groves watched the drummer boy's face as he planted the seed to keep things quiet. He knew Leroy would do anything to keep his favor. He was young and impressionable, and looked to Groves as a father since his real one had left when he was born. Leroy looked at Groves and walked toward the door. "Yes pastor, I understand, I know how to keep things private. I always do." With that, he walked away. Groves went into bathroom to freshen up before going home.

Michael was different than his father; he hated the thought of cheating. It was never much of a secret that his father cheated and that his mother knew about it. She never showed much emotion; maybe it was due to the hurt and pain she had endured while watching him disrespect her and the church. Countless women, some from the church, others from the street; it never mattered as long as they were willing. She always remained loving and forgiving, but in maintaining the façade of forgiveness, she had grown emotionless. Michael grew up longing for his mother's love and receiving his father's adoration. When he met Vhannie, he finally had both. She loved and adored Michael. He loved her as well. The couple was rarely seen apart. The years of his father's infidelity, however, had taken a toll on Michael. He had adopted some peculiar interests, one of which involved sex toys. They had a great sex life, but even the best of relationships needed some spice every now and then. He loved his toys, movies, and especially his dolls. The first time he discovered his predilection toward dolls was when Vhannie had gone out of town. He had done well the other times she left on business trips, but this time was different. They had spent most of that Friday morning before her flight making love, but on Sunday, he was horny again. He called her hotel room that morning before church to engage in some very sexy pillow talk. She was good at saying just the right words and injecting a sigh and a moan at the right time to keep him hard and his hand busy. But after the 1-900-style call was over with his wife, the fire had not been quenched.

That Sunday he paid more attention than normal to the sisters on the front row. One in particular he knew would have been on her knees at a moment's notice if he had asked, but his distaste for his father's behaviors prevented him from acting on his desires. After church he went home and watched online porn. There was a doll on one of the adult sites that looked more human than anything he'd ever seen. The online company even allowed him a preferred skin color. They offered all ethnicities and when he looked at the African American ones, there were even more choices: from the darkest of chocolate to the sweetest caramel. At first he thought he'd get two, one brunette and one blonde. Why not?" he thought, "A ménage-a-trois." It would be a wonderful Sunday night. His life with dolls began that night. Later, it would end with them.

Peoples looked at the files on his desk and wondered where the answer lay. He read the report on Michael's death and shook his head as he read the coroner's findings. Heart problems, clogged arteries, high blood pressure and ultimately a heart attack. "Okay," Peoples thought, "I'll buy the clogged arteries and the high blood pressure, but someone initiated the heart attack and it wasn't a damn doll! What?" he thought, "What am I missing, why can't I see it or read it? Surely its here, somewhere in these papers!" He felt the answer lay hidden. Then there was the small man, was there a connection to him among the papers? Why was this man murdered? Could the man somehow be connected to Michael's murder … to David

Jacobs? All of this was just too strange, yet it had to be connected, he just couldn't figure out how yet. Peoples thought, "What do you do when you got a puzzle, you put the pieces in that you know fit and work the rest of them later, after the picture comes into focus." He continued to read and lost track of time.

ABDUCTION

A black Ford Explorer was traveling down a neighborhood where small children played. The driver slowed to take a look. He smiled as he looked at the little faces, all innocent and sweet; he began to rub himself and spotted the one he wanted. A little girl about five years old played by herself on the sidewalk. The driver pulled closer to get a better look and to make sure no parent was around; the child was alone. He smiled as he let his window down, "Hi, sweetheart, are you having fun….would you like to go get some ice cream? Where is your daddy?" "I don't have a daddy," she said as she approached the truck. "You don't? Wow, that makes me feel bad. You know what?" She shook her head. "I know where he is," he said. "I can take you to him. Would you like to see your daddy?" The little girl looked puzzled and happy at the same time. "You know my daddy? Can you take me and my mommy to see him? My mommy said she hasn't seen him since I was borne, she lost him." "I can't take your mommy, but I can take you, wouldn't it be great to surprise your daddy, and then when you come back you can tell your mommy that you found your daddy!" The little girl started jumping up and down and then the driver opened the door and pulled the little girl inside the truck.

The occupant in the dirty apartment sat next to the phone looking at it as if by sheer will it would ring. It didn't. There would be no phone call, no one to check in with, and no one to direct the plan. All decisions now would rest with one instead of two ... no partner, no one to pass blame onto if the plan failed ... Well it couldn't fail, and from now on, things would be different.

Peoples' was headed to Vhannie's apartment when he got the call. A little girl, five years old, was missing. He pulled his car over to the side of the road carefully, not wanting the sound of the tires on the pavement to interfere with the news of the missing girl. The girl was about 3' 7" tall and weighed 42lbs. She had long brown hair with a missing front tooth. She was last seen wearing jeans and a Hello Kitty t-shirt with pink tennis shoes. The mother confirmed the little girl had been playing just outside the front door and that she had just checked on her before going inside for lemonade. The girl's mother was being interviewed by the local news channel and appeared somewhat apprehensive as television camera closed in on the house where the little girl was last seen. People's called into the station and got directions to the little girl's house. Although he wasn't assigned the case, he wanted to go and watch the events. Somewhere in the back of his mind, he felt he needed to be there; that being at the scene of the abduction would help his own case, or at least get his detective juices flowing again. He felt he had gotten off track with Jacobs and needed to re-energize his efforts in catching him. The entire neighborhood was on edge, parents and children alike were outside holding each other and crying. Police cars were parked in front of the mother's house and now a second television crew had arrived.

It was organized chaos in the neighborhood that was already always busy with people coming and going. The mother, who had appeared shaky while being interviewed, now stood quiet and strong as a tall, husky man who had arrived earlier held her in his arms. Peoples stood among the neighbors, listening to the chatter, hoping to overhear something that would help the police bring the little girl home. What he heard made him angry. "You know I'm not shocked that little girl got snatched up like that, actually it's a wonder it didn't happen sooner." One lady with an infant in her arms chatted with another tall lady who was standing next to a police car. "Yeah, me too. Well you know she never paid any attention to that little girl ever since her old man left, now look at them, standing there like June and Ward Cleaver with all those television cameras on them. They're trying to make people think they are some kind of close knit family." "But you know what makes me madder than hell?" the lady with the infant said, "Where was all these damn police when they was selling drugs from that house? Hell, if they had come then, maybe little Kayla would still be safe. You know they could have found her some parents who really care, not these fake wannabes crying like they really care." The tall lady shook her head in agreement and then turned and noticed Peoples standing beside them. "Do you know them?" asked the lady. "No," Peoples replied, "I'm just here trying to see what I can do to help. I was wondering if maybe the police or the husband might organize a group to canvass the neighborhood." "Humph," the lady said, "the husband ain't gonna do nothing but wait to see how much reward money they gonna offer to find Kayla. He's worthless!"

Peoples walked away from the two ladies, saying he wanted to get closer to hear what the police were saying. He moved over to one of the police officers he knew well and asked if they had anything yet. The officer said it was too early, that the child had only been missing for about five hours, but due to the rash of missing children, the captain wanted a police presence on the scene for the television crews. The amber alert had gone out and no one had seen or heard anything. Peoples stood looking at the family, remembering another time and another little girl. That little girl was found but it was too late. And if what the ladies had said was true, Kayla was another little girl born to the wrong parents.

Kayla cried silently as the man molested her. Over and over again he touched her in secret places parents warn their children about. Kissing her face gently and licking away her tears, he told her everything was okay. He told her that what he was doing was what every father does to his little girl when he wants to show how much he loves her. Since she had lost her father, he would take his place and show her love. The little girl cried and moaned, her small body wracked with pain. It had been over five hours since he had pulled her into his truck, now it was over and he was taking her back home. The girl was quiet, whimpering as he drove to DQ to get the ice cream. He went in and she lay curled in a ball on the back seat. When he returned, she refused to accept the ice cream turning her head away toward the window and looking out, crying softly that she wanted to go home. Jacobs told her that she should eat the ice cream because he promised it to her and he never breaks his promises. She continued to look away, silently crying, asking to go home. Jacobs was sure there would be police everywhere if he tried to take her back home, so he drove to a park two miles from her house where there were teenagers hanging out, drinking beer and smoking weed. He left her on a bench in the park. He smiled at her and told her that everything would be okay. Then he looked at her again and said, "If anybody asks you about me, you should say you don't remember anything, 'cause if you do, I'll come back and take you away again and you'll be lost just like your dad." Then he drove away and the little girl cried on the bench for her mommy.

Peoples walked around the neighborhood, listening to the gossip about the little girl's family. Once he thought he overheard someone say the mother had been known to smoke crack and might have exchanged the child for drugs. This infuriated him and he got in his car and drove away. He headed back to the police station to look up information on the mother and father. He needed to know for sure that this little girl was not being mistreated by a couple of drugged out low-life's. He spent the next few hours searching rap sheets and any type of domestic charges on either parent, what he found was typical of drug users; a few charges, and a couple months in jail for possession and Child Welfare called out at least once every year of the little girl's life. She hadn't been treated like a princess, but she hadn't been neglected either. Peoples decided to head home and call Vhannie once he got there. Stank had been home almost all day. Even though he was a good dog and never had any accidents in the house, he wouldn't be surprised if he'd had a mishap. This one would be forgiven. He was driving home when he noticed a black Ford Explorer going in the opposite direction … Jacobs? Peoples almost stopped in the middle of the street. Why didn't he think of Jacobs earlier today? As soon as he heard the amber alert on little Kayla, why didn't he think Jacobs? He made a U-turn and followed the black Explorer; it turned into David Jacobs' driveway.

Jacobs got out of the car with keys in hand as he made his way to the front door. As soon as he entered the house, Peoples went up to the truck and tried to peer into the windows. The tint on the side windows was too dark, combined with the night, to get a good view. He walked around the back of the truck hoping the hatch would be unlocked; it wasn't. He bent low and looked at the tires, hoping to find a leaf or a twig or something stuck to one of the tires. He looked at the front wheels and then the back without any luck. All of a sudden he heard voices and the light went on in the yard. He hurried back to his car and waited for the voices to subside. When the coast was clear, he went back to examine the car again. He looked at every inch of the truck and just as he was about to walk away, he spotted it. There was a small piece of paper lying on the ground beside the driver's door. It looked like some sort of receipt. It was white, with a date, time and store number printed on it. It was for two cones of ice cream from DQ. Peoples grabbed the receipt and headed for his car. He didn't know what the receipt meant, but he knew it was one piece of the puzzle. He would need more before he could start putting it together, but at least he had one more piece.

Vhannie turned over in her bed looking at the clock on the radio. She grabbed her cell phone and checked it for messages from Peoples. He had not called or texted. She began to get worried. She went into the kitchen to get a glass of water, when she heard noises that sounded like someone was outside. The nuts from her trees had begun to fall, and sometimes they landed on the roof so loudly it sounded as though someone was trying to break in. She dismissed it and returned to her bedroom. The sound came again, this time it was not the sound of nuts hitting the roof. Instead, it sounded as if someone was pulling on the doorknob, trying to open the door. She went to the armoire and got her pistol. She had bought the gun after the bank robbery. Peoples had convinced her to take the concealed-carry class so that she could carry it with her wherever she went. She was a good shot and not afraid to use it. If someone was really trying to come in, she would make sure they would stay in … dead on her floor. The wrestling with the door knob grew louder. Vhannie inspected her gun to make sure it was ready, took a stance, and aimed toward the door. The sound stopped as abruptly as it had started. She stood still; ready to shoot any intruder who might try to enter her home. She let out a sigh and then readied herself again to shoot. Expecting to see a big, burly man dressed in black, she moved closer to the door. She took a deep breath and flung the door open, pistol cocked and finger on the trigger. She peered into the darkness for the man dressed in black. The night was still, except for the sound of crickets and the neighbor's dog. She closed the door and went inside to call Peoples.

Peoples had just closed his front door, letting Stank out to relieve himself, when the phone rang. "Hello, Lang? Lang, are you home?" Vhannie sounded scared and annoyed on the other end. "Yes baby, I'm here, what's wrong, what's going on?" "There was someone trying to get into the house, I got my gun and aimed it at the door, then I opened it and no one was there, but I'm sure someone was trying to get in, I'm not crazy or anything and I know the difference between nuts falling on the roof and someone shaking the door knob trying to open the door! I think they thought

I wasn't home and maybe they would have come in if I hadn't been here. I would have shot them dead if they would have tried to come through my door!" "Yes, baby I know you would have cause you're a hell of a shot and you know how to take care of yourself." "You're damn right, and you know what else, let them come back if they want to, you'll be investigating another murder case." Peoples smiled underneath his breath, letting her vent and agreeing that nobody in their right mind should try to break in her house. "Baby," he said, "do you want me and Stank to come over?" "No," she said, "I'm alright. I just wanted you to know that's all. Are you in for the night?" "Yes," he responded, "I think this has probably been one of the most confusing days I've ever had. I am so tired; I'm going to crash if you're okay?" "Yes, babe, I'm okay. I'm going to bed too and I'll call you tomorrow at lunchtime." Peoples blew a kiss into the phone and they both went to bed.

Kansas City went on with business as usual. Traffic jams continued to cause commuters to be late for work, people stood in line at the DMV and the bank continued to turn down people with bad credit. Vhannie loved her job, but hated all the politics. Meeting after meeting, she'd listen to the comments and complaints about this and that. Everyone wanted to shine, all jockeying for position, for the next promotion; managers agreeing to every proposal and nodding in unison at how great the presenters were. There were VP's and AVP's, Directors and Supervisors, Senior VP's and CEO's. COO's wanting to be CEO's and VP's watching AVP's making sure they stayed in their place. The room was full of titles, the people part had gotten lost along the way, the people part remained at the branches with the tellers and the new accounts representatives, or the phone reps and the maintenance workers. Everyone who attended meetings did so because they were the brightest and the best, the movers and shakers, they were also the ones who were stressed and kept a copy of their resume in their desk drawer. They were told they were leaders and that they should be independent thinkers, as long as the thinking didn't question the status quo. Thinking was good among this group of intelligent, hardworking leaders, so good at times that real change happened, even if it took years to occur. Often times the idea would be revered as new, not because it was new, but because someone new presented it. That was how things got changed, one person with a less important title offered a suggestion, then years later someone with a bigger title offered the same suggestion, then it was accepted. Vhannie watched as the same people were selected time after time to sit on focus groups to test new software, offer suggestions and test for problems. The reality was the people selected were chosen because they asked the questions the top leaders could answer without having to appear unprepared. It was like watching a Republican rally with the standard person of color strategically placed where the camera, no matter the angle, would capture them in the shot. Whether you believed in the project or not, you had better not speak against it. The way to keep your job was to agree, and if you had concerns, you should start your sentence by saying. "I can see the benefit of this," or, "this is an excellent idea to move us forward … I just need more clarification on this or that." Vhannie had learned to play the game and she had gotten pretty good at it. She knew the right things to say and when to say it. At times she even got the proverbial pat on the back for her ability to find new ways to do things. The one thing she couldn't seem to do was get the next promotion. So she continued to do her job while waiting to find out who killed her husband...

She missed Michael and the life they had planned. The nights when in bed they talked about growing old together, and traveling to Africa had now become a distant dream, unfulfilled just like her life now. So she focused on her job and on Peoples. He had always been important to her, but when they first met, he was too arrogant and insensitive for her to consider him. They played around and had great sex, better sex than she and Michael, and Peoples never needed any toys to get in the mood. All he ever needed was the idea, and it didn't matter where it came from. A sexy thought that she often provided for him with a phone call, or just driving toward her house, he always seemed ready. He had his preferences too and some included role playing. She knew that by playing along with the game she was condoning the behavior, but she also knew it stroked his ego, and if stroking his ego gave her the pleasure he provided, she would continue to stroke it every time. They played around for years until she wanted a commitment, something he told her he could never offer. So when Michael Groves proposed, she accepted. She loved Michael, just not in the passionate way she adored Peoples and now she was involved again, all because of the robbery at her bank, or the death of Michael, she didn't know which excuse she wanted to believe.

A CITY IN TROUBLE

Sometimes the city becomes its own person, with emotions, aspirations and failures all jumbled up and fused together. Kansas City was a person with growing pains, disappointments and sadness, sometimes overwhelmed with joy and hopeful with dreams. When the sports teams won, the city was youthful and spirited; everyone liked each other, Black, White, Hispanic, Asian and Arab, old and young, rich and poor, Democrat or Republican, differences were moot and winning brought everyone together. Laughter and Barbeque, beer and red jerseys could solve any world problem. So it was not surprising that the city became sick and listless when the little girl was found and the news reported how she was abducted in front of her house; carefree and young, she had become another statistic of the carnal nature of the city. No medicine prescribed could cure the sickness of the city, it was chronic and contagious.

The Mayor spoke to the citizens and assured them that the sickness would be contained. He knew better than to say it would be cured, for he knew that the sickness of the city was a sickness the world had produced and only the world could cure. Parents listened closely and discussed with their children the need to stay close, never interact with strangers, and to remember to scream and run away if someone attempted to grab them. Children played and listened to their parent's fears, wanting only to be children without fear and restrictions. The police continued to be vigilant, and worked crimes as they happened. Peoples became more and more interested in Jacobs, less and less interested in Groves. It had become a cold case, yet he reminded himself that he needed to get it solved … after he caught Jacobs. He was convinced Jacobs had been grabbing little kids and doing unimaginable things to them; he was also convinced he would get to the bottom of it.

When the little girl returned home from the park, the parents immediately called the police. The teenagers who delivered her answered all the detectives' questions although they were of little help. One of the teenagers, a young woman around 17 years old, was the only one who actually saw Kayla crying on the park bench. She took her jacket off and covered the little girl as she called her friends over. After an hour, the little girl was able to tell the teenagers where she lived, and they took her home. "We never saw anyone with the little girl," the teenager said, "all I saw was her, and actually I heard her before I saw her. She was crying, not very loud, but loud enough that I looked around, trying to locate the sound. That's when I saw her on the bench." The parents were pacing back and forth in the living room where the detectives where questioning the teenagers, Kayla sat on a chair with a stuffed animal in her arms staring at the floor. Her body seemed to be smaller than before. The police called an ambulance and, after the paramedics checked her out, took her to the nearest hospital for a thorough exam. The doctor talked to the parents first, giving them life-altering news: Kayla had been molested, a rape had occurred. The detectives were given the news next and, although they had seen the worst the world could throw at them, they never handled the news of crimes against children well. They took the little Kayla and her parents home, then went to the nearest bar.

Peoples looked at the receipt in his hand as he drove home. The day had gotten away from him and he felt he hadn't accomplished anything. The drive home always settled his mind, especially when it was 80 degrees and the wind blew warm against his face. He drove the route to his house the same way for years, never really altering it as he had been taught; he liked the sameness about his drive. His life as a detective had enough changes and surprises, so driving the same way every day was one constant he could rely on. The other was his dog, Stank. He loved that big old lump of a dog; if life got too hectic, or his faith waivered, he looked at Stank and it seemed to put everything into perspective. He often wondered if Stank ever got tired of doing the same old thing, a dog's life was full of constants: eating, pooping, chasing a squirrel or cat, sleeping and an occasional belly rub, was about all Stank could hope for. He had been fixed, so there would be no little lumps running around. Peoples smiled as he pulled into the driveway of his house. When he opened the door, Stank jogged toward him and pushed his big head against People's leg. People's rubbed his head and asked him how his day was. Stank looked at Peoples as if to say, "You know how my day was, it was easy."

Peoples began taking off his clothes and made his way into the kitchen to make a drink. He turned on the news to see

Kayla's parents on the news holding the little girl's hand, and looking sad and tired. The teenagers who had rescued the child were being interviewed, but Peoples turned the sound down. He poured scotch into a glass with two ice cubes and a shot of 7up. As he went in to run a bath the doorbell rang. He looked at the clock on the wall and decided it had to Vhannie, but it was not like her to not call first. She didn't need to, but that was the way she did things. She explained to him that calling first showed manners, and she didn't ever want to run into someone else at his house; someone else like another woman. Peoples went to the door and looked through the peep hole; it was dark and he couldn't see anyone. He called out, "Who is it?" There was no sound, then a knock. "Who is it?" he yelled. Peoples walked back into the kitchen, got his gun from the holster, and then went back to the door. Stank seemed to appear from nowhere, headed for the door as he growled, ready to do battle. Peoples made his way to the front door, gun aimed as he flung it open only to find no one there. A car door opened in his neighbor's yard as a couple got out and headed inside the neighbor's house. Peoples and Stank walked around the house, looking for the source of the knock on the door, but there was nothing and no one, the area was quiet. Stank continued to search around the back of the house and into the neighbor's yard, smelling and sniffing for a clue. After a few minutes he made his way back to the house. Peoples wondered if had been imagining things. He had been working a lot with the Groves case and the surveillance on Jacobs; he decided he was just being paranoid and need to rest. He and Stank went back into the house and he settled into the bath. Stank curled up alongside the tub and stared at the door.

Jacobs went into his basement, and into a small room he had built for himself. No one had ever been in this room, his wife never knew it existed, and if the kids wandered anywhere near it they were quickly distracted and headed off in another direction. He had installed a special lock that opened by biometrics, controlled by his palm. This was his sanctuary, and the place that allowed him to feel special. He walked around the small room, quickly making an assessment of everything, determining that nothing had been disturbed. He opened a cabinet and pulled out a small case containing pictures, small pieces of paper, ornaments, and small bottles. The pictures were of children; playful, smiling, happy times, always taken in front of their homes. The papers were usually receipts of where he'd taken them. He liked to visit places like McDonalds, DQ, or any fast food restaurant where he could use the drive-thru and pretend he was the Daddy and the children he had stolen where his children, being rewarded for good behavior. Sometimes he'd keep a barrette, or toy car, or soldier, anything his victims had when he grabbed them became his to keep. His most cherished items, though, were his bottles. Jacobs called his bottles 'Innoscents'.

When he took his victims he would capture their tears on a Q-tip and place the tip into a small bottle. Then he would add scents he identified from the capture and place them into the bottle. In his warped mind, he was recreating the innocence he had stolen. With little Kayla, he noticed the clouds that evening were full of rain, so in her bottle along with her tears he added the smell of rain. Jacobs had found a company that sold scents which represented nature. Scents like rain, snow, heat, grass, sunny days, nights, or any other smell he could associate with a moment. It was difficult at times, because his requests were not always scents the company could reproduce, so he adapted his request and began asking for several different scents, and in this small room he combined them in mixtures that produced the desired effect; reminding him of the moment of his attack. His plan was to one day market his perfumes of 'Innoscents' to people longing to recapture their days of childhood and innocence. He figured he would make lots of money and no company would be able to figure out the secret ingredients, making reproductions impossible. He would take special orders from customers and, depending on what the request was, he would get a child, capture their tears, add the smells of the moment the customer remembered and produce the perfect product. Ingenious, he thought, and he was well on his way. In his case he had already produced 50 bottles; not enough, he thought, to start his business, but once he reached 100, he would start accepting on line orders, making 'Innoscents' the perfect gift.

He reached into his pocket for the receipt from his trip to DQ with Kayla and found only cotton. He stood up, searched both pockets, and looked around the room hoping the receipt had fallen out and was on the floor. Realizing he had lost the receipt, he panicked. He stood still, rubbing his neck and trying to recall his last steps after dropping Kayla at the park. He tried to remember if there had been other stops between the park and his house. He recalled only pulling into the driveway and getting out of the truck. "That's it!" he thought out loud, realizing the receipt was probably there. He closed the door behind him, and headed to the driveway.

Peoples awoke feeling refreshed and new, happy that his phone had not rang in the middle of the night alerting him of another homicide. Kansas City was on target to break a record for homicides and both the mayor and the police department were trying everything they knew to stop the senseless killings. Gun buybacks and sporting events scheduled in the inner city did little to halt the tide of crime. Young black men were killing each other at alarming rates and, although clergymen and councilmen were all looking for answers, the real answers were found in the broken homes of single mothers raising young men without the benefit of a stable, mature male figure. The homes of these confused and hurting young men were often-times filled with equally hurting young women who started motherhood all too early. Unfulfilled promises of love and protection were replaced with desertion and denial; denial of paternity. A shortage of money to buy Pampers and food and pay for a decent place to live left many mothers on Section 8 and in neighborhoods were everyone lived the same way they did. So little innocent black boys grew up with other little black boys whose futures mirrored each other and whose lives were shortened.

When a young man was found shot to death, the family of both victim and killer often mourned alike. The difference between the two was separated only by time; killers often met the same fate, often within months, or days of the crime perpetrated. So the police tried to replace years of pain and feeling less than human, with basketball tournaments and speaking engagements at local high schools. Community activists patrolled neighborhoods and asked area businesses to donate to community centers that sponsored all kinds of sports camps and extracurricular activities, anything to harness that painful negative energy into positive outcomes. Some participated and tried to escape the violence, only to go home and face the reality they felt outweighed the ninety minutes of hope the centers provided.

Young mothers, sometimes only fifteen years their child's senior, were still having children and looking for the man who would stay and help provide for their growing family. But these men, being asked to provide stability and promote fatherhood, were at a disadvantage since they had no reference to draw from. So the cycle continued, and young black men were becoming an endangered species. They city couldn't solve the problem because the problem was bigger than the city, the police force and all the city councilmen and community activists combined. Instead, they opted for a Band-Aid to stem the bloodshed; they patrolled the areas of the city where the need was greatest. The mayor and the police reached out to the clergy, and they walked the streets, organizing vigils with former gangbangers there whose lives had been changed by long stints in prison, or by time. Grandmothers and mothers grieved openly and begged for the murders to stop. The killings, however, continued. Peoples was thankful he'd been able to get a good night's rest, but he knew the day would bring him back to reality. He drove to the station and started his day.

Jacobs looked around the driveway, along the curb and even into the grass to locate the receipt. When he couldn't find it, he became angry; not at anyone in particular, but at the possibility that he had failed to keep something so precious to him and his impending business. He went back into the house and into his room. His mind was racing as he retraced his steps from the night he abducted Kayla. He pulled the bottle of 'Innoscents' that held her memory and put it back into his case. He felt better knowing he had captured the smell of that night and held the bottle tightly in his hand. The receipt was nothing; really, it was only a memento along with countless others. When he first began his quest to capture and bottle innocence, he thought of keeping small items to recall the event, but after watching an infomercial where the pitchman was selling personalized dolls, he had an idea. The dolls were replicates of the individual requesting it, they simply provided their own clothing, pictures and perfumes, and the company was able to produce an exact replica of that person. Jacobs thought it was a great idea; all he needed to do was alter it a bit. Instead of producing an actual thing, he would produce a moment, a scent that captured a moment in time. "What a great idea," Jacobs thought.

He felt illuminated and aroused as he decided to incorporate the idea of personalization with his ongoing desire for children. Scents of his captures bottled up like the most expensive perfumes, allowed him to relive each moment. It was after the third bottle that he got the idea of turning his growing need into a business that he knew would appeal to almost anyone. Everyone had a moment in life where they were at their happiest, especially when they were children, and he was a mad scientist who would give the world the ability to go back in time via their olfactory nerves. He smiled, put the bottle back into his case, and decided to take the family out for pizza.

Kayla's parents called the police station and asked for Peoples. When the call reached him he was surprised, and hesitated to take it. Why were her parents asking for him, he wondered; he had not been assigned the case and had not been present when the teenagers had returned the little girl. For all they knew, he was just another overworked detective fighting a never-ending cycle of crime. He answered anyway, curious for something that would indicate how they knew, and why they were requesting, him. "Hello is this Detective Peoples?" the child's mother asked. He answered cautiously, "Yes, this is Peoples, how can I help you?" The mother responded that she had been asking for him since the abduction and was met with a lot of resistance. "I was wondering if you could tell us how the case is going." Peoples explained that he was not assigned the case, the detectives assigned were very competent and he'd be more than happy to get them on the line. "No!" she pleaded, "Please detective, don't pass me along. I know you're not assigned to my baby's case, but I also know you care more about Kayla's case than anyone. I know who you are and what you are. I know what kind of man you are, and that you were at my house the night of the abduction. I know you were around asking questions, so you see, detective, I know that you are working my baby's case even if you weren't assigned to it." Peoples tried to disguise the surprise he felt at how much she knew about him. He sighed into the phone and told her that at the moment he would not be able to talk to her. She knew what he meant, and asked that he find some time to visit Kayla. She told him that she felt there was something her daughter wanted to say about that night but no one, not even the detectives assigned the case, could get her to talk about it. Peoples said goodbye and hung up the phone. He felt in his pocket and pulled out the receipt from DQ he'd found in Jacob's driveway. Tomorrow he'd visit with little Kayla, but tonight he'd visit Jacobs.

The dirty apartment had been cleaned and the person who had been two and now was one prepared to go. He drove to the bank and asked to be let into his safe deposit box. The teller asked for ID and led the man in. Vhannie had just returned from lunch when she noticed the man entering the safe deposit area. She smiled at him and went into her office. As she sat down, she had the distinct feeling she'd seen the man before. It was a strange feeling; not like someone you'd seen millions of times and couldn't remember their name, instead it was a feeling of someone you'd only seen once or twice, or seen on the news. It was a feeling that said this was someone you knew or had heard of, and it made her uneasy. She pretended to be busy as she waited for the man to exit. After an hour, the man appeared and quickly walked out the door. Vhannie tried to get a good look, but he left so quickly she'd only been able to see a glimpse of him. She got up from her desk and asked the teller to give her the folder of the man she'd let into the safe deposit room. She read the name and hesitated; the last name was Nubote. She didn't recognize it, but that was not unusual, she managed a large branch and had over three hundred safe deposit boxes, most of which were rented at some time or another. Then she went into her office and tried to locate his account information. She found out the account had been open less than 6 months and the man had no other services with them. She looked again at the file and then located a picture. He had provided an out of state driver's license and the description on the license was of a black male, 5'9 inches tall, weight 185 lbs. The address made no difference to her, except he had lived in Florida. She still felt uneasy and wanted to know more about who this man was. It was a strange feeling she had, and it was one she couldn't shake.

The man noticed the manager and wanted to run to his car when he saw Vhannie. He'd been in the bank on at least four other occasions and had never run into her. He began to worry that she knew him. He felt she shouldn't't' know who he was; there was no reason for her to. But he wasn't sure if she'd make the connection to why he was there. He made it to his car and began looking through the documents from the safe deposit box before leaving the parking lot. As he inspected them he smiled when he located the papers he needed. He drove to the bus station and looked around for her. Lying on the ground with an empty bottle beside her, the woman appeared to be dead. He stood over her and watched her chest for any sign of life. Then he saw it; a slight up and down movement, she was breathing. He called her name, "Josey! Josey, get up."

PUZZLE PIECES

The feud between Huber and Groves had taken on a life of its own. Everyone had an opinion, and no matter whose side was being represented, it all got blamed on Josey. Groves had built one of the largest churches in Kansas City. With a congregation that rivaled any mega church anywhere, Greener Pastures was the place everyone in town, at one time or another, called their own. Some in the city went to see if they could find where Groves had been buried. Each Halloween, kids would dress up as preachers and go to the church pretending to be Huber; they would apply makeup that simulated a hole in the head. Others would dress as Groves and lay on the ground while their friends pretended to pour dirt on them, simulating his burial. The adults liked to talk about how a sexy woman who used to be a man was able to destroy the best friendship ever between two men. No one ever questioned why the two, who had shared the same dream, became rivals before Josey entered the picture. To talk about that would not be as juicy, it was much more interesting to talk about a man who became a woman and who by all accounts fooled an entire congregation, not just Huber. The city gossiped and kept the ghosts of Huber and Groves alive. The death of the younger Groves couldn't begin to gain the popularity his father and his father's rival had. Although his death had the same air of impropriety about it, it just didn't interest people the way the elder Groves' had.

As the city talked and reminisced about the former best friends, now both dead, the investigation of Michael Groves' murder stalled. Even Peoples, whose job it was to investigate the murder, seemed to rate it as least important on his scale of crimes to be solved. He became anxious to visit Kayla's parents and decided Jacobs could wait for now. As he drove to the house he started to think about the night of the abduction and what the neighbors had said about the parents. He knew there had been some drug abuse, and one time where little Kayla had been remanded by child protective services, but there was nothing that indicated they would have been involved in her kidnapping. No, he thought, they weren't Clair and Cliff Huxtable, but they weren't the worst parents either. He decided to go and see if he could get Kayla to talk about the night someone took her away. He had the receipt in his pocket and maybe if he showed it to her, it might jog her memory. His phone rang, it was Vhannie. He hesitated to answer it, not because he didn't want to hear from her, but he knew if he did, he'd find it difficult to get off the phone and get his focus back on Kayla. So he let it ring and go to voice mail. He'd call her back later, after he had a chance to talk to the child. This was an opportunity of a lifetime and he knew it. He didn't want to blow it. Somehow he knew this meeting would be another clue that would get him closer to catching Jacobs. He hadn't connected him to the abduction at first, but now things were starting to add up. There were many pedophiles in the area, and any one of them could have done this, but somehow he just had a feeling it was Jacobs. The son of a bitch was slick, but not so slick he wouldn't be caught.

Vhannie called again, this time Peoples looked at the phone and got a little worried. It wasn't like her to call back-to-back, something was wrong, and he was tempted to answer it. His mind started imagining all sorts of things; what if someone was trying to kidnap her, what if she had been robbed, or raped? What if the crime was happening at that very moment and he could stop it … he answered. "Hello," she said, "are you very busy, something happened today at work and I need to come by later to ask you some questions." "Oh," he sighed, "yeah babe. I'm in the middle of something … are you okay? You say it can wait until tonight?" "Yes," she said. "I'm sorry I got you at a bad time. Go ahead and do your thing, I'll meet you at the house later. I'm gonna go get Stank and take him to the doggy park. Bye, babe." Peoples smiled into the phone and hung up. He looked around and realized he was pulling up in front of the house. He waited a few seconds, composing his thoughts before entering. He knew Kayla was fragile and the parents frustrated, so his approach had to be just right. So much was riding on the success of his interrogation of the child. He hated thinking of it as an interrogation but, for lack of a better word, that's what it would be.

He made his way to the front door and the mother greeted him with an outstretched hand. "Hello Detective, thank you so much for coming. I know my call was unexpected, but I knew you'd receive my request. I just don't know what to do at this point. Everything seems to be falling apart. She won't sleep by herself, won't go outside, she doesn't like being in any room by herself. And she cries most of the time. Not huge tears running down her face, it's more like pain pushing through to the surface and it streams down her face in a trickle … it's so sad to see Detective … my heart breaks each time I look at her face and realize I can't help her. I can't help my little girl; do you know what that feels like? A mother not being able to protect their child?! It's hell!" Peoples just listened as she unleashed her own pain. "I can't tell you I know how a mother feels, and no, I don't know what it feels like being unable to protect your child, but I do understand hurt. Hurt comes in many ways, and what I can tell you is that I live with it each time I have to inform a family that their loved one has been killed. It may not be my child, but I do feel the pain and unlike yours, which is terrible, just imagine having to deliver that pain over and over again for years. I'm sorry Mrs. King, I'm very sorry."

She turned to the sofa and invited Peoples to sit. Little Kayla appeared with a doll in her arms and went to her mother. She looked so tired, more tired than any five-year-old should be. She tried to muster a smile when her mother asked her to say 'Hi' to the nice Detective. "Hi Kayla," Peoples smiled at her, and asked who the friend she had under her arm was. "This is Jade, she's my doll. She's pretty and smart, just like I used to be." Her mother looked at Peoples as if to say, 'See? Now you see her hurt?' Peoples said, "Hello Jade, and yes she is very pretty and smart. Kayla, you are not only pretty and smart, but you know what else you are? You are strong. Do you like dogs?" Kayla nodded, yes. "Well, then let me show you a picture of my dog, Stank." Peoples pulled some pictures from his wallet and showed them to her. "See, this is Stank when I got him from the shelter, he was so small and cute, don't you think so?" She nodded her head and took the picture in her hands. "Now look at this one, this is him now that he's all grown up. He's still cute and you know what else? He's really strong and smart. He is big and strong and very smart, and I think he's the cutest dog ever." Peoples looked at her to see if the pictures of the dog affected her in any way. She took the other picture and starred at it for long time. Then she placed Jade beside her and looked at the detective and began to smile. "I think he's the cutest dog in the whole wide world."

"I wish I had a dog," she looked up at her mother, "cause if I would have had a dog, the man wouldn't have gotten me. My dog would have chewed him up!" Peoples smiled and said, "You know what? I think a dog is a great protector, just like a mommy and a daddy. Your mommy is so worried about what happened that she asked me to come and talk to you. Can I ask you about the man who took you away?" The child nodded as she gazed at the picture of Stank. "Did the man that took you away, did he take you somewhere where you got a treat? Did he offer to buy you something?" She looked as if she would cry, and then said, "Yes, he took me to get ice cream because he said I had been a good girl." Peoples was excited, but made sure he didn't show it. She looked at her mother and started to whimper, "I don't like ice cream anymore mommy." Peoples began to leave but noticed that she still held the picture of Stank in her hand. "Would you like to meet Stank?" he asked. "Could I?" she smiled. "Can I keep his picture until you bring him over? Can we play together, me and Stank? Maybe I can take him for a walk?" She looked at her mother. Peoples looked at the both of them and said "I'll bring him by on Friday, how's that?" He left both pictures of Stank with the little girl, and headed to get Jacobs.

The man and Josey went back to the apartment. He looked at her with disgust, trying to understand how she had allowed the pressure of what people said destroy the beautiful person she was. She walked in and flopped down on the sofa, coughing as she sank into the cushions. As she looked around trying to figure out where she was and who the man was talking to her, she started to laugh. She had been a strong woman, beautiful, vital and non-compromising. Growing up as a man and then becoming a woman took 'balls' she'd say, "And I do mean it took balls…where they took them to, who cares!" Now she was broken, drunk, and sad. She had been through a lot since Huber had killed himself.

At first she went back to St Louis hoping to start life over, but it was not to be. When she arrived she met a man who offered her a place to stay and told her she didn't have to work; all she had to do was keep the house clean and look pretty. She could do that she thought, and for six months it worked … until the day when she went shopping, and forgot the time. When she walked in the door with bags in hand, he knocked the bags, and Josey, to the floor. The next thing she knew he was slamming her head into the wall, spitting in her face and yelling that her responsibility was to cook, clean, and be there when he got home. He continued to hit her until she was unconscious. When she awoke he was standing over her with a skillet and a pot, and told her to 'get her ass in the kitchen'. The next day, she waited for him to go to work, packed her clothes, and took the next bus to Atlanta. When he got home, he looked around the apartment, calling out her name, waving a small bag in his hand. Josey was nowhere to be found. When he looked in the closets, he realized she'd left him. He fell down on the bed and took the box, containing an engagement ring, out of the bag.

In Atlanta, Josey fell in with a small group of transsexual and transgendered people. The leader of the group was a transwoman named Jeanie who owned a clothing store. Josey had been window shopping when Jeanie approached her and invited her in. She asked her if she needed a job, because she thought she looked lost, although she was dressed very nicely. She said she needed someone who could bring a little class to her shop. Josey accepted the job and they became very close. After a year, she told Jeannie that she had been engaged to a preacher in Kansas City who committed suicide when he found out about her. Jeannie shared stories about the heartbreak she'd encountered, and soon after, they moved in together. The one thing Jeannie had not shared was her addiction to drugs. When Josey found out, Jeanie at first swore it was just for recreational use. Then the parties were every Friday night, and the drug use became more frequent. Josey resisted for a month or so, but one night, when she'd been stood up for a date, she decided to try it and her life went into a tailspin. Everyone they hung around was either transsexual or transgendered. Josey felt out of place because she didn't fit in either group. She was a woman as far as she was concerned, and made sure nobody got her confused with them. Most of the group liked her, but felt she thought she was better than them because she had transitioned.

Her addiction took her places she'd never seen. She began working as a call girl, then taking on clients who engaged in S&M. One night she took a call from a john who wanted to be with her and another transsexual. She agreed, and met the man at a hotel. She and her friend entered the room, and began negotiating prices when the man asked her if she would cry for him. Josey, looking confused, began to laugh, asking the man to repeat what he'd said. He asked her again if she would cry for him. He looked at her and handed her an extra $300.00. Her friend offered to cry, but the man said he didn't want his tears, only Josey's. She sat on the bed and began thinking about Huber and the life she would never have with him, and the tears flowed. The man reached into a case and pulled out a Q-tip. He touched the tip to her cheek and then placed in inside a small bottle. She dried her face, and began to get high.

Peoples drove to the Jacobs house and parked across the street. He looked at the receipt in his hand and remembered the story Kayla had given; 'yes we went and got ice cream because I had been a good girl'. This so-called business man, who wins awards and dines with the mayor, molests children. Soon it would come to an end, and he would make sure Jacobs spent the rest of his life behind bars. It was getting dark, and soon Jacobs would come out and begin his hunt. This time Peoples would follow him, maybe even approach him. Jacobs came out of the house and got into his truck. As he pulled away, Peoples followed. He was close, but not so close that Jacobs would have noticed he was being followed. Jacobs drove for about twenty minutes before heading into a neighborhood where a few children were hanging out. The dark truck slowed, taking in all the sights and sounds of the children laughing and playing. There was one little boy, about 6 years old, playing fetch with a small dog. Each time the stick was thrown a little farther, each time the dog retrieved it and brought it back, causing the little boy to laugh out loud. Jacobs parked his truck directly across the street and watched the innocent play, waiting for his chance to grab the little boy. Peoples parked on the other side of the street about half way down the block. He began to snarl and growl as he watched his prey. He realized he was getting overly emotional, and needed to calm down if he wanted to catch

Jacobs and not compromise his investigation. He crouched low in the car and rolled down his window. The little boy continued his play, but this time the dog didn't bring the stick back; instead he looked back at his young master and continued to run, wanting to be chased. The little boy went after his dog, laughing and calling its name.

Jacobs started his truck and made a U-turn in the street, driving slowly, following both dog and boy. Peoples waited and didn't move as he watched Jacobs drive past him. The little dog kept running and so did the little boy. Jacobs drove close to the little boy and started to chat with him. "Hey, need help catching that little rascal?" The little boy looked surprised, never realizing he was being followed, but noticing he had run too far. The little dog was still running so he continued to go after it. Jacobs pulled his car over to the curb and got out. "Let me help, he said, I'll get him for you, you stay right there, okay?' The boy didn't know what to do; continue to run after his dog, or stay where he stood and wait for the stranger to bring him back. Jacobs quickly rounded up the little dog and started to walk back to the boy when he heard someone yelling for the boy to come home. It was his mother and she was walking down the block toward her son, yelling at him to get back to the house. "Forget about that dog!" she screamed, "Get back to this house!" Jacobs cursed under his breath and put the dog down. The little boy had made his way close enough to Jacobs that he could have been snatched up easily. The little boy grabbed his dog, looked at Jacobs, and then ran back toward his house.

Peoples crouched low in his car as he watched events unfold. He felt his anger subside, then felt relieved. He was sure now that Jacobs was behind the abductions, and he had almost caught him. He watched Jacobs get back into his truck and drive away. He followed him until he pulled into a gas station. Peoples waited to see if he was going to buy gas or go inside. Jacobs got out of the truck and went inside; Peoples followed. He made himself a fountain drink and headed toward the checkout when Peoples stepped in front of him, almost bumping into him. "Sorry, man," Peoples said, and asked the cashier for two lottery tickets. Jacobs looked at him and smiled, "It's okay, go ahead." Peoples paid for his tickets and was about to leave when a uniformed police officer stopped him, "Hey Peoples, what you up to tonight?" Jacobs looked at him and made his way quickly to his truck. Peoples played it off and started chatting with the cop. Jacobs drove away and headed back to his house.

As he drove home, the child molester began wondering about the cop who had just bumped into him, and if it meant anything. He started thinking about the little boy and the dog and how close he had come to grabbing him. He wondered if he was just being paranoid and the cop being at the same gas station at the same time was just a coincidence. Cops were at that gas station all the time and running into one was as common as getting a speeding ticket at the end of the month. There was nothing to it, he thought, and he chalked this one up to a coincidence. Just in case it wasn't though, he wanted to remember that name, the name the uniform cop called the guy who almost bumped into him, "Peoples … yeah, that was it." He found a pen and a piece of paper in the glove compartment when he got to a stoplight, and wrote the name down. He would remember him next time, and the next time the two of them met, he would make sure Peoples knew who he was.

JOSEY AND LEVAR

Peoples began to think about what happened at the gas station and wondered if Jacobs knew who he was. He was sure he had not been recognized even though he had staked out Jacobs' house several times, and they never exchanged a word at the ceremony. Because the uniform cop had said his name, he knew Jacobs would be on guard whenever they made contact again. He needed to get down to business and catch Jacobs before another child was kidnapped and their young lives turned inside out by his disgusting actions. As he drove home to meet Vhannie he wondered what had gotten her so anxious. She could be a little dramatic at times. Most women were, he thought, but something else was going on. No one on the force knew about his relationship with her and he liked to keep it that way. He preferred to keep his private life, private. The gossip and cheating that happened at the station was something he wanted to stay far, far away from.

He pulled up in the driveway and saw her car. When she called earlier and said she needed to talk to him about something that happened at the bank, he was a little hesitant to hurry home. His chance encounter with Jacobs made him itchy; he wanted to follow the bastard and catch him right then and there and be done with the whole affair. He opened the door and found the house empty. He looked for Stanks' leash, it was gone. So he took his shoes off and made himself a drink. The door opened and Stank jogged over to him, nudging his hand as always so that he would scratch his head. Peoples obliged the big dog and kissed Vhannie on the forehead. "Hi baby, how was the walk?' "Good," she said, "how was your day?" "Oh, you know, nothing to talk about, same day same crime." He took a big sip of his drink and walked into the living room. "Did you feed him babe?" "Yes, of course, but he wanted a snack when we went for our walk, so I gave him a few too many treats." "That's okay, anything for my man." Peoples felt Stank brush against his leg as he lay down on the floor. "Now you come over here and tell me what's got you so excited.

Vhannie sat down next to Peoples and pulled some papers from her brief case. "Look at this picture and tell me if this person looks familiar to you." Peoples stared at the picture and rubbed his chin. He looked again and tried to compare similar faces from his memory. "Should I know this character?" he asked. Vhannie didn't answer his question, instead she told him to keep looking. He looked again and said, "Well, do you want me to run his license?" She took the picture away from him and looked into his face, "Doesn't he look like Huber?" Peoples looked again at the picture and began to access the facial structure; the forehead, nose, high cheekbones, slim mouth, and then he looked at Vhannie. "Huber, Pastor Huber, who shot himself in the church parking lot after his wife to be, was found out to be a man? That Huber?" "Yes," she said, "that Huber, only younger, say, 25 years younger?" Peoples looked again at the picture, pretending to see the resemblance. "Hmmm," he said in between drinks, "I never knew Huber had a son, hell, I never knew he had *any* children. So if this is his son, who is the mother, surely Josey isn't. What was he doing in your bank?" "He has a safe deposit box," she said, "and apparently he keeps some very important things in it. When I looked at his entrance file, I noticed he'd been in it over 4 times. I never knew Huber had a son either. Michael never mentioned him and I don't think he was ever seen at the church. Surely someone knew about him, but I wonder why he has been such a secret, and better yet, why is he here now?"

Peoples took another sip and recalled the day's events. The phone call from Kayla's parents, the information about eating ice cream with her abductor; the receipt from DQ found in Jacobs' driveway, the attempted abduction of the little boy, and now the appearance of someone who looked like Huber; it was all too much and if there was a connection, he didn't know what it was. The detective gods were smiling down on him and he was being favored. But what to do with it all, he hadn't yet figured out. Then he remembered the man found shot to death at the apartment and the pictures he'd confiscated. The puzzle was still in the box and now it was time to put the pieces on the table and try to put them together.

He went to his garage and retrieved the bag that included the picture and clothes he'd kept from the homicide of the unidentified man. He took his findings and laid them on the kitchen table. Vhannie came in and put the picture of the man who looked like Huber on the table with the rest of the pieces of the puzzle. They looked at each other and back at the items on the table. Neither said anything for at least twenty minutes, picking up the pictures, examining them and then laying them back on the table. Peoples looked at the torn fabric from the pants and back at the picture of the family. He looked at Vhannie and smiled. She smiled too, although she didn't know why

Josey lay on the sofa in the apartment while the man who had rescued her paced back and forth asking questions about why she would allow herself to live like a piece of trash. She could tell he was talking to her, but her mind was so foggy she was not clear on what he was saying. She knew that whatever it was, it wasn't good. She tried to prop herself up, and cleared her throat enough to ask for a glass of water. He looked at her with disgust, but went into the kitchen to get it. She moved from the sofa to a chair in the room and sat upright taking in the apartment. There wasn't much to look at and she had the impression the person getting her water hadn't planned on staying at the apartment much longer. She began to feel ill, and her body ached from lying on the ground. She asked for a blanket as he handed her the water. He went into the bedroom and returned with a blanket and a pillow. He told her that she should lie down. He moved toward the bed and pulled the covers down, and Josey got up and went to the bed. Curling herself into the fetal position, she looked up at the stranger and then fell asleep.

Peoples grabbed the pictures from the table and went into his office. Vhannie decided to go into the living room so that he would not be distracted. She could have gone home but being by herself these days did not appeal to her. She looked at Stank and decided they would just hang out together. So she turned the television on and began watching detective shows. Peoples began searching online for anyone with the last name Huber. He did a 'people search' through every search engine he knew of. Although he could search through the police's database, he sometimes found that doing searches online through non-police databases produced very interesting things. He loved Face book and Twitter and had used both social mediums with excellent results. He typed in Ken Huber and waited; pictures of men from Michigan, Illinois and California all with the name Ken Huber were staring back at him, but none who looked like they would be the son of a man who had died over twenty five years ago. He used the first name of the deceased in hopes that Huber would have wanted a junior. He looked at each man and carefully examined the face of each one, looking for something in the eyes or nose, or the way they smiled to indicate a resemblance. He read each profile hoping for a connection to Kansas City and the pastor … he found none. He was thinking fast and typing faster. He decided to type only the last name to see what he would get. Nothing, no one, not one hit! Peoples smiled, he was never one to give up so he decided to do something else. He typed in Josey.

Bingo! There she was; beautiful, sexy and 100% female. There were pictures of Josey posing in all the latest fashions. She was smiling and happy in each photo. There were several people with her in a few photographs. Peoples could tell that some were probably transgendered, but they all looked happy and were having great fun. The background for one picture looked like a clothing store. He looked closely at the picture and read the caption underneath … it was a clothing store in Atlanta. He read the name: 'Fierce Fashion'. He quickly did a search for the store and went to the website. The clothes were top notch designer, trendy and expensive. There was a picture of the owner, her name and a phone number for contact purposes. Peoples wrote down the information and put in his jacket pocket. He would call her tomorrow from the police station and ask her about Josey. He felt better, having decided he had one more piece of the puzzle. Hopefully he'd find a connection after he spoke to the owner of the store.

Vhannie was still in the living room when she heard Peoples call. She got up and walked in the bathroom where he lay in the tub full of bubbles. "Wanna get wet?" he asked. She smiled and began to get undressed.

Jacobs was not in a good mood since he had been unsuccessful in his part-time job, kidnapping and molesting children. He was short and curt with his wife, and even nastier to his children. He lay on the couch in the living room pretending to be interested in a football game when he got a phone call. He excused himself and went to his secret room and sat down. The man on the other end began telling him that they knew who he was and, although one had been killed, he was himself still alive and well. He told Jacobs that he was not afraid of exposing him, nor was he afraid of being shot and killed like his partner. Jacobs was quiet and said nothing to the person on the other end. He was surprised, shocked and irritated at the threats coming through the receiver. The person continued his tirade on Jacobs, saying that in due time the two of them would meet and then he'd see that he was no one to be messed with.

The phone went dead before Jacobs could say anything. He got up and took his case form the locked cabinet. He pulled out one, then two of his bottles. Jacobs did not label any of the bottles, for he knew who and what they represented. Just the mere smell when the cap was removed was enough to bring the memory back to him. He inhaled deeply the scent from one of his most recent captures; Kayla. The smell immediately aroused him and he closed his eyes. He sat for several minutes remembering how he grabbed her and how she cried. Then he remembered how he had touched her cheek to capture her tear on the Q-tip. He also remembered how he dropped her off and left her on the park bench. He smiled and touched himself until he exploded.

The next morning Peoples found himself anxious to get to work. He kissed Vhannie and horsed around with Stank before making his way out the door. He felt energized and excited like he was twenty-five again. He didn't need any pills or energy drinks; all he needed was the energy he got when he knew he was close to catching a criminal. After his online search last night and the discovery of the clothing store in Atlanta where Josey had worked, he was sure he would find some answers. He was on cloud nine and ready to get down to the business of catching criminals. He was out the door and in his car when he got the first call. A woman was found dead near a school on the south side of the city. This was not how he wanted to start his day, but if a dead body was on his list of things to do, then off to the school he went.

He arrived and found the body of a white woman in her early twenties lying on her back with what appeared to be bullet holes in her upper torso and her legs. She had been shot numerous times and was naked from the waist down. She was very pretty and appeared to have been in pretty good shape. Her top was very short and showed a lot of cleavage with two tattoos, one on each breast. Her pants were found only a few feet away. They were skinny jeans and looked as if they had been ripped off her body. She had shoulder length blonde hair and some hair was found around her head as if someone had pulled it out. Peoples looked closely at the hair and discovered they were extensions. Then he noticed a piece of paper in one of her hands and took it out to read it; it was a parking ticket from a downtown parking garage next door to a gentlemen's club.

The ME arrived and began making his assessment of the body. Peoples walked toward the other detective at the scene when he got the second call...

Jacobs was nervous and excited as he drove through the neighborhood where children played without a care in the world. He knew it was risky trying to get a child early in the morning, but he was getting desperate and couldn't wait until nightfall. His desire was stronger than his ability to contain it. He had tried to satisfy his need by pulling out a different bottle each night for the last few nights and allowing the scent to satiate his desire. It was not enough. This morning, then, he went to look for a child instead of going to work. Jacobs decided that if he went into the inner city, he'd have a better chance of getting a child no one would miss. He found a little boy about six years old alone and crying next to an old house. The boy was oblivious to the man driving slowly as he pulled up to him. Jacobs smiled and asked him if he'd missed his bus. The little boy turned to look at Jacobs and said yes. He said he was in trouble because his sister wouldn't wait on him and left. He asked Jacobs if he could take him to school. Jacobs said yes and the little boy got in.

The school reported that one of their students had not arrived. The little boy's teacher was nervous when her star student had not gotten off the bus. She went to the principal's office and asked to speak to the boy's sister. The little girl explained that Levar had been messing around this morning and was going to make her late, so she left him. "He should have gotten on the bus with me," she cried, "He probably went back home!" The teacher, Ms. Jenkins, called Levar's mother and asked if he was home. His mother said no, he should be at school. "He's not there?" she screamed into the phone, "Find my child, please!" The teacher ran outside and began searching through the busses lined up by the curb. When she couldn't find him, she told the principal to call the police.

The call Peoples received was about another missing child. He should have continued to investigate the tattooed dead girl; instead he headed toward the elementary school.

Jacobs was done with Levar as he touched his cheek with the Q-tip to capture his tear. The child cried but was defiant as Jacobs placed the Q-tip into the bottle. He looked at Jacobs and asked him why he didn't take him to school. Then the boy asked when he was going home. Levar stared at Jacobs and wiped the remaining tears from his face. He looked around the room to find something he could take back with him. Jacobs was busy organizing the bottles, making sure the newest one was securely in the case, and never noticed the child pick up a discarded Q-tip, quickly placing it in his jeans pocket, as he waited for Jacobs.

They drove around for what seemed like hours. Finally Jacobs found a spot to let the little boy out. It wasn't close to where he had grabbed him, but close wasn't important to Jacobs. He needed to find a spot that afforded him privacy and seclusion. Levar was quiet and never looked at Jacobs or through the window to know where he was. He focused on the Q-tip in his pocket. He remembered a television show that advised kidnapped victims to try and keep something from the assailant. He didn't know what an assailant was, but he remembered an after-school class on safety and knew he had been assaulted. Jacobs finally found a row of houses that looked as if they had been in decay for some time, but were fully occupied. There were cars parked in front of two of the houses, so he knew if he let the little boy out someone would find him. He drove around the block until he was sure no one had spotted him, and then opened the door, let the boy out, and drove away.

Peoples arrived at the school and met the teacher, the principal, and the mother of the missing child. The police were asking questions of everyone and anyone who had been on the bus that should have carried Levar to school. Peoples asked his own questions because, although missing children were not his business, any child in danger was. Yes he was a homicide detective, but he had made a commitment to helping find missing children ever since the Precious Doe case. Regardless of what anyone said, he knew why he was there and he was thankful he had gotten the call. When he spoke to the mother, he found out that Levar was left alone by the bus stop because his sister had gotten angry at him for playing around and she didn't want to miss her bus. Both mother and daughter were hard to understand as they spoke through tears. His teacher had almost collapsed as she leaned against the wall of the school repeating the child's name. She was overcome with fear as she begged the uniformed cops to "Please find my Levar…please find him."

News cameras were everywhere as elderly homebound citizens stood around shaking their heads and acknowledging the decline of society. Other parents who had been called by their children were arriving, and the chaos worsened. Peoples looked around and took notice of license plates, year, makes and models of the cars parked on the street and in the teacher's parking lot. He needed to run the plates, and clear any not worth pursuing. If he got a hit, then he'd turn it over to crimes against children. He was stressed and angry, a feeling he liked because that was how he got things done. Some people worked best when they were calm. Not Peoples, he needed the adrenaline and he got it when he was stressed and angry. The dead body by the school, the missing boy and the discovery of the clothing store in Atlanta, had him wound up. He was super-charged and ready to check things off his list. First things first, he thought, he needed to head to the station and find out who the pretty dead blonde was. But on his way, he'd drive by Jacobs' house.

When he arrived at the house, Jacobs was nowhere to be found. The house looked empty and almost void of any signs of life. The wife and kids were gone and the neighbors were all locked in their homes. Peoples parked up the street and walked down to the house. He walked up the drive way and peered into a window. He had no idea of what he hoped to find, just for some reason he felt he needed to. He wanted to look into the life of a pedophile, the most vile and evil thing on the face of the world. He wanted to look into his world and understand what drove him to become the lowest form of human life. He hoped to find some sense of normality and the one thing that made him the monster he had become. Peoples wanted to make sense of something senseless and maybe he would see it through the window. He saw nothing.

The police station was buzzing as phones rang, citizens made complaints and police wrote reports. The dead blonde girl was identified and the next of kin were being contacted. Peoples walked in and sat at his desk. He pulled out the DQ receipt and began calling to find out which store it had come from. He discovered the store was about thirty miles away from the police station and decided he would have to wait and visit them when he had time. Right now he had to deal with the murder of the young blonde. He had the ticket from the parking garage he'd taken from her hand and decided he would make a trip to the gentlemen's club.

THE BUSINESS OF SELF HATE

Downtown was still trying to rebound from years of urban flight and, although condos and lofts littered the streets with fancy names like "Chicago Place" and "Park Avenue North" penetrated the skyline, most city folks longed to be suburbanites. They came equipped with high end appliances, exercise gyms and concierge services. Some of the young and eager who had been lured to Kansas City for jobs liked the downtown experience. They were smart, eclectic, eager and shared none of their parents' ideas about city living. After all, most big towns knew they needed a thriving downtown if they were to compete for the big conventions. Every year large organizations looked for the top spots to host their national conventions. A town needed to have tourist attractions, sporting teams (all the better if they were winning), five-star restaurants and hotels, low crime and competitive prices. Kansas City, MO had most of that before the flight to border state Kansas.

Kansas had been able to snatch away some of the best attractions, like the soccer arena, and the Legends, with one of the largest furniture retailers as its anchor tenant. A large theatre chain's home office moved to the state along with a premier cell phone carrier all calling Kansas home. With so much to offer, it wasn't hard to understand why the affluent moved westward. Now Missouri had to rebuild itself, so it launched the Power and Light District, with numerous bars and restaurants nestled closely together in an eight-block radius. It brought NBA basketball to the Sprint Arena, along with major concerts and any other form of entertainment one could see in cities like New York, Chicago, or LA. For the more refined, Kansas City built the Kaufmann Center with its ballet, symphony and Opera performances; there was something for everyone who ventured downtown.

Some visitors liked a downtown that grooved like the funky 70's and nothing was more funky than slab of ribs and a side of beans from a downtown BBQ restaurant and soul food joint. For the less uppity refined down home folks, Kansas City had Gates BBQ and 18th and Vine, former home of the Negro baseball league. Visitors and Kansans alike got their BBQ from Gates. So when Peoples went to the gentlemen's club and found out the pretty blonde danced at the club and lived in one of the lofts along Broadway, he was not surprised. She had been one of the young and eager who didn't share her parents fear of the big bad city, but maybe she should have because she lay cold and alone in the morgue. Peoples asked to speak to the manager of the club and was introduced to a man with a thick Spanish accent. His name was Jorge and he was from Guatemala. He told Peoples he had only been the manager for less than 1 year, but he knew Cindy well. She had started out as a customer who came in with a man about once or twice a month. She'd only begun dancing about six months ago and had done pretty good for herself. When Peoples asked who the man was she had been seen with, Jorge said that he hadn't paid much attention to the man, only that he remembered he was a small man who seemed out of place in the club. Peoples asked if Cindy had been seen with anyone else, a boyfriend perhaps, or anyone possibly related to her, maybe a customer or two who liked her and wanted more than a dance. Jorge said he hadn't known of anyone she had complained about. "Cindy was just a real sweetheart and she was such a pretty girl, she was really too nice to be in this business," he told Peoples. "I used to ask her why she was dancing, and she always said she liked to dance, that was all to it."

Peoples jotted down the address and numbers of everyone Jorge said he knew she had told him about. He talked to a couple of the other dancers and got the name of her last boyfriend although the girl who gave it to him quickly explained that he couldn't have done it because he and Cindy had broken up over two months ago and she had been seeing him. She and Cindy's boyfriend had started messing around and that was the reason he and Cindy broke up. The two of them had gotten into a fight. Donnie, the ex-boyfriend, had been in jail for the last couple months. She was waiting for him to get out because they were getting married. Peoples left the club and went to get some BBQ.

Levar was sitting in the yard as a man emerged from one of the distressed houses. He looked at the child and called out to him, "Hey, hey what you doing in my yard?" Levar stood still as the man approached and began to cry, "I want my momma!" the man asked him who his momma was and what his phone number was,

Levar gave him his mother's name and phone number. The man began to call the number on his cell phone, when his wife came out of the house. "Hey, hey what's going on, whose child is that?" She asked. The man told her he didn't know, that the child was standing there crying for his momma when he walked out the door. His wife walked down to the yard and looked at Levar, "Come in the house sweetheart, let me get you a blanket and some water, then I'll call your momma." She told her husband to call the police, while she went inside and called the child's mother.

Levar's mother was the first to arrive, followed closely by Peoples, who sat across the street and watched. He didn't want to get in the way and respected the detectives who handled child abuse cases. He waited in his car as he ate his BBQ sandwich. The boy's mother and sister hugged him tightly and kissed his face. He cried as the police took him to sit in one of the police cars. They took child, sibling and mother to the police station and began asking questions, careful not to agitate or cause Levar to shut down. He responded well to the questions, offering a description of the man and the fact that he drove a big black truck. He also told the police the man was large, white and had bad teeth. When asked what the man did to him, Levar began to cry. Immediately his mother interrupted the questioning, asking if they could allow them to go home and possibly talk to him on another day after he'd had a chance to feel safe again. The police obliged and drove the family home. Peoples remained at the scene asking the family who had called the police, if they had gotten a chance to see anyone in the neighborhood they didn't recognize. The wife told him no because they had been in the house, and people drove around that neighborhood all times of the day and night. The father stated how he had walked out to get in his car, when he saw Levar. He didn't recognize the child from the neighborhood, so he began asking him who he was. Then the wife came out and told him to call the police. Both husband and wife were visibly shaken as they recalled the morning's events. Peoples never showed any emotion as he listened to the pair, but inside he was seething with anger. He knew deep in his bones Jacobs had grabbed the little boy. He would visit Levar after he'd had a chance to calm down and realize he was no longer in danger. Unlike little Kayla, Peoples wouldn't wait on an invitation from the parents, he knew he needed to act fast.

Levar sat in his room staring at the toy soldiers and cars he'd gotten for getting good grades. His teacher, who constantly told him how smart he was, had bought them. His mother loved the fact that his teacher liked her son so much, she was grateful that both her children had good teachers. She had been having a hard time ever since their father had to leave for his third tour of duty. She worked as a customer service agent for a large insurance agency and her hours were the same as the school's hours. In some ways she was lucky because she didn't have to pay for someone to watch them while she worked. She knew of several mothers whose husbands were away and how they struggled to pay for childcare. It was difficult at times just to pay for food and rent. So when Levar's teacher offered, actually insisted, on buying toys for him, she gratefully accepted them. Toys were a luxury that she just couldn't afford. There had been other times when the teacher had helped her with groceries as well. She had developed as close a relationship with his teacher as her son had.

Levar studied his little soldiers as if to make them move. He picked them up, one by one and, stared at them. "Why didn't you come to save me?" he asked. "You're a soldier, you have weapons like my daddy, but you didn't come to rescue me, why?" The toy was still in his hand, with a glassy stare that gave nothing away. "I don't think you're a very good soldier," he said to the toy, "you are just worthless!" His mother stood in the door way as she watched her son wrestle with the pain of being snatched away from her. She cried under her breath wishing she could rewind the day. She wished she would have made sure both her children were safely aboard their bus before she headed off to work. She would have kissed him longer and admonished her daughter to never leave her brother no matter how late they would be. She would have made breakfast instead of telling them to fix cereal. She would have done a lot of things differently, but most of all she would have kept him safe from harm, because that's what a mother does. She looked at him and suddenly realized he was looking back at her.

Peoples knocked on the door and the interruption startled the mother. She quickly wiped her tears away and headed to the door asking the intruder to announce who they were. Levar came out of his room and went into the kitchen to get a butcher's knife. His sister sat on the sofa pretending she was watching television. The mother looked to see if Levar had stayed in his room and noticed the knife in his small hands. She went to him and tried to get it away, but he struggled with her as he cried saying he needed to protect them from the man who took him away. His mother told him it was okay, no one was going to hurt them ever again. There was another knock as the little girl jumped from the couch and yelled out, "Who is it?" Peoples, realized they were probably afraid to open the door, so he yelled through the door and asked the mother to go the window and look out. He held his badge up to the window and told them he was a detective.

The door opened slowly, as both children stood beside their mother. Levar still had the knife in his hand as Peoples stood by the door. "Hello, my name is Detective Peoples, this is my badge and this is my license. Would you like to call the police station to verify me?" The mother hesitantly took his badge and examined it carefully. She then looked at him and said she remembered he was at the school earlier in the day right after they'd called and reported Levar missing. "No," she said, I believe you. Peoples noticed the knife in the small hands and the eyes that looked like they had aged twenty years in one day. "Hi Levar, you look like you could really hurt someone with that knife. I bet you could really protect your family if you had to," he said, "but I'm a police officer and I wouldn't hurt you. My job is to protect you and your family. I was too late to protect you from the bad man who hurt you, but if you help me, I'll catch him and put him in jail. Do you want me to do that?" Levar looked at Peoples and looked at the badge. He examined it and looked back at Peoples. "Okay, you can stay, but remember, I have a knife and I know how to use it." Peoples moved slowly toward the sofa and sat down. He took out a notebook and a picture of Jacobs taken at the mayor's celebration posted in the newspaper. He smiled at Levar and asked him if he remembered where the man took him. The little boy shook his head and said no. Peoples told him that was okay, and then he asked if the man had taken him to get ice cream. Levar looked surprised and shook his head no. Peoples told him how brave he was that he had stood up to the man and that that was the reason he had let him go. Levar looked at Peoples and nodded, as if to say he agreed that he had been brave. He asked Peoples if he knew who the man was that took him away. Peoples said no, but he would find him. Levar asked him how he was going to do that because he didn't even know where the man lived. Peoples told him that finding people was what detectives were good at, and he was a very good detective. He told Levar, “I found out where you lived, right?” The boy looked as if he had just figured out the hardest math problem on a quiz. He walked over to Peoples and whispered in his ear, “The man took me into a room and he touched me privately, you know, where men aren’t supposed to touch you.” But I got this from his room. He fished in his pocket and pulled out the used Q-tip and gave it to Peoples.

He walked back to where his mother had been watching silently and sat in her lap. Peoples took the Q-tip and placed it in a tissue he had in his pocket. He knew evidence was supposed to be placed in brown paper bags, but he didn’t have one, so he wrapped it up and put in his pocket. Just as he was getting up to leave, he decided to show the little boy the picture. “Levar, would you look at this picture and tell me if you have ever seen this man?” The little boy wouldn’t get off his mother’s lap, so Peoples walked over to the two of them and showed the picture. Levar’s face changed instantly as he tried to talk thru tears.

“That’s the man! That’s the man!” Peoples quietly exited the house.

Peoples slammed his hand in the door as he entered his car, cursing as he sat behind the wheel. His emotions shifted between anger, excitement and an overwhelming desire to go to Jacobs’s house and drag him out by his hair. The thought of Jacobs doing things to Levar and other children made him clench his teeth and slam his other fist into the steering wheel before starting the car. He needed to slow his accelerated heart beat and the thoughts racing through his mind. He needed to ground the rage that coursed through his body. No matter how he looked at things, Jacobs needed to be caught soon, and right now was as good as anytime.

He knew he didn't have enough to arrest Jacobs. A piece of cotton swab and an ID from a 6-year-old child could put Jacobs under suspicion, but it wouldn't be enough to put him away forever. Forever is what Peoples wanted. He wondered if Kayla would be able to ID Jacobs. He was sure she knew the man who grabbed her from her house, but young children were easily confused. Sometimes make believe and reality were not very different for a young child, and to put them through even the most remedial interrogation was more than Peoples wanted the children to deal with at this point. He needed to do more, and make sure that when the time came to have the children testify about what happened to them, it would put the nails in Jacobs' coffin. Both children had been seen by therapists, combined with social workers who had been assigned the case. The results of the medical test taken at the hospital had not yet been released and, because he was not the lead investigator, he had to wait until all the evidence had been collected and evaluated. In the meantime he needed to figure out the importance of the cotton swab along with the receipt for ice cream and put the pieces together in some logical form.

He headed back to the station and listened for any information regarding Levar's kidnapping. He knew the detectives who were working the case and wanted to ask them if they had a suspect, but he knew he needed to work his own cases, one of which was trying to find out who had killed the young dancer found dead at the school. He reviewed his notes several times, wishing the words would somehow create a clearer picture of the suspect. They did not, though Peoples read them again and again. He knew that, hidden in every conversation between police and citizen, there was a clue to what and who was responsible for every crime. Sometimes it was what the witnesses said, other times it was what they didn't say. It was funny how people carefully chose words when being questioned by the police. It was that carefulness that created the sense of doubt: things were not always as they appeared. A husband, whose wife has been missing, never admits to fights and affairs and is always very careful to describe the relationship as loving and caring; yet he waits a week to contact the police. When questioned, he says how much he loved her, not how much he loves her! A fight between two friends who have never had an argument results in death, only to find that one hated the other and had always been jealous; jealous enough to kill.

Peoples looked at the pictures of Cindy lying dead on the concrete parking lot and the picture of her dancing at the club. He remembered Jorge saying she was often seen with a small man. He wondered who the man was. Was he a sugar daddy? He wouldn't be the first man who paid for the company of a beautiful young woman. Or was he someone she knew in a different way. Was he related to her? He needed to pay a visit Cindy's parents.

Josey woke up and looked around the room for the young man who had rescued her. She got up and walked around the apartment, looking into the bathroom, realizing she was alone. She looked around for pictures, or anything to help her identify the stranger. She was surprised when he found her and brought her here. He spoke as if he knew her well, but she hadn't recognized him, and she wasn't sure if she had ever met him. Maybe he was someone from her past, or someone she knew when she was turning tricks. He didn't look like someone from the streets. She knew the streets and how it could turn an otherwise simple, straight-laced, hard working person into something unrecognizable. She had been a good, kind and easy going person, until her life changed. Once she left St. Louis and moved to Atlanta, she became the kind of person others ignored. She got caught up in a world of drugs and prostitution and became the kind of street person she herself had always shunned. It had started slowly at first, dabbling in cocaine, smoking weed and partying. Her friends were able to maintain their habits, limiting their use to weekends only, but not Josey. Once she got high, she wanted it every day; it made her life without Huber easier to manage, or at least helped her forget the life she thought she was supposed to have. Jeannie had tried to help her kick her habit, but Josey didn't want to. She continued to work at the clothing store in the daytime and as an escort at night to fund her habit. One day after several hundred dollars went missing, Jeannie confronted her and told her that she either get help, or get fired. She loved Josey dearly and would have never had her arrested, but she thought the threat of termination would be enough to make her go into rehab. It didn't work, and Josey found herself without a job and without a good friend. She began escorting full-time and her drug habit escalated. She was arrested several times, but it never took the desire for the drug away. She found herself meeting very strange men and, sometimes, even stranger women. One day she met a man who knew her from her days in Kansas City, and after they were done exchanging favors for money, he asked her to cry for him. She found the request odd, but complied as he touched the Q-tip to her cheek.

Josey went into the kitchen and returned with a glass of water. She sat on the sofa just as the door opened and the young stranger appeared. He looked at her and asked if she'd had a restful nap. She nodded her head and sipped her water. He went into the bathroom and returned with a camera. As he sat down in the chair opposite her, he asked her if she would allow him to take her picture.

She looked puzzled and a little frightened. She didn't know what his intentions were, but at that moment she looked like trash and felt worse. Why he would want to take her picture was puzzling. She attempted to smile and asked why he wanted to take pictures of an old woman like her. He looked at her and said that she wasn't that old, but that he needed to take a before shot of her, because for the next few weeks he was going to help her return to the beautiful woman she once was. Taking the picture now, he assured her, was necessary because soon she would only have the photo and her memories to remind her of what life had done to her. Josey tried to straighten her spine as she sat upright on the sofa. She asked for a mirror and a comb to fix her hair, but before she knew it, he had snapped the picture.

ALL THE PLAYERS

Sometimes things happen for reasons no one can explain. Like when two people meet for a date. The physical attraction can be so overwhelming that a chemical reaction takes place which renders both parties helpless. An attraction between two people that others view as odd, or unusual, leading to a connection so strong it can only be broken by death. Such connections are puzzling when they don't fit society's standards. We judge spiritual connections by physical standards. Tall should be with tall, short with short. Fat should only attract fat and beauty should always be adored and protected. Old should go away and pitter patter around the house, while young finds itself laughing and dancing the night away. We create our own social prisons and then fight to get out of them. Cindy fought against all the stereotypes heaped upon her and tried to help others bound by the same chains.

Going away to school was for her parents, not her. College was not what she wanted and soon she found her way out and into the gentlemen's club, dancing and feeling sexually free. Her introduction to the club came on a warm Sunday afternoon while walking her dog. She sat on a bench, resting in the sun's rays. Seated on a park bench next to her was a man who looked as if he were the only person in the world. He'd noticed her before she came close to him, catching a glimpse of her and hoping she had not noticed him. She was young and beautiful, not someone whom he could ever hope would look at him, but she did. She caught his gaze and sat down beside him. They began to talk and all of society's norms were broken. The aged man and the young beautiful woman formed a deep connection that perplexed minds and made mouths wonder aloud. He took her to the club not because he wanted to, but because she wanted to go. She wanted to dance, and she did after about a month or so of going and watching the other girls. She danced and seduced men with every twirl on the pole. She danced in laps and took her money to the bank on Mondays. And one day, she was found dead in a school parking lot.

Peoples pulled up in front of the home of Cindy's parents and walked slowly toward the front door. A reddish-brown Great Dane greeted him as he rang the doorbell. The glass door opened into a modest home complete with just the right amount of furniture and pictures of happier family times. Cindy's father invited him in while her mother entered with a picture of Cindy from middle school. She was young, eager and happy, surrounded by friends who only knew the world from their limited time in it. She was their child, all fourteen years of her; with a fate no one could have predicted awaiting her. Peoples smiled as he took the picture and declined the offer of coffee. He looked at the two of them and offered his condolences as the Great Dane made his way toward him. The wife attempted to correct the dog's advances, but Peoples patted his head and gave his blessing to the greeting. Cindy's father began to speak about the life path Cindy had taken, starting with the failed attempt at college and ending with the unhealthy relationship she had with the man who had introduced her to the club scene. His wife nodded in agreement at every disappointing decision the father felt Cindy had made. Neither was able to come up with anything good their little girl had done after she dropped out of school. It was as if she was someone they never knew or ever wanted to know. She had become something they thought happened to others, certainly not them. They were both college educated, bright, financially responsible adults who gave to charities. They voted Democrat, were pro-choice, and for equal rights for gays and minorities. They had voted for Barak Obama and had the bumper sticker on the Mercedes to prove it. They attended church regularly and had sex once a week. They had one child and she had been planned. Before Cindy was born they both attended Lamaze classes together and took a 3-month leave from their jobs when Cindy arrived. Their lives were orderly and planned from the moment they met in college to the day they heard the news their only child had been found murdered. Peoples listened and asked about the first boyfriend; if they knew him well and what they thought of him. The father responded no, they didn't know him or where he or his family was from. They had only seen him once when Cindy had dropped off some cookies she'd baked. He had driven her over, but never came in the house. He waited in the car, parked in front of the house instead of in the driveway, her father quickly pointed out. The mother looked at Peoples as if to say, can we get on with this? She never spoke a word the entire time he was in the house.

Peoples asked them what they knew about the man Cindy had been seen at the club with. Her father went into another room and returned with an old Polaroid of a man, a woman and a couple of children. The picture looked like any family who might have been gathered outside their home on a sunny day. Cindy's father told Peoples he thought the man in the picture was the man Cindy had been dating when she was dancing at the club. Her mother nodded in agreement and handed the picture to Peoples; they agreed he could keep it.

When he started the car, he decided it was time to go home and put the day's events behind him. He called Vhannie and told her to meet him at his house. She arrived first and let Stank out as she looked around the house making sure everything was in its place. She went to the kitchen and began preparing dinner. The freezer was bare except for some ground turkey and chicken wings. She looked in the cupboard for anything that resembled vegetables and found a can of green beans. Then she assembled spices and ingredients to make a meatloaf. Peoples always liked her meatloaf. Although he was a pretty good cook himself, he preferred her cooking. Vhannie liked to cook and she loved to bake. So once she put the meatloaf in the oven and prepared the green beans with potatoes, she looked for baking items. She was good at substituting items to make a dish. She found flour, cinnamon, peaches, butter and shortening. "Mmmmmm," she thought, "this looks like a peach cobbler!" and soon it was in the oven. Peoples arrived to the smell of home cooking and a big wet nose as Stank greeted him. He kissed Vhannie on the cheek and slapped her on the butt. She smiled and told him she had run him a bath. He stopped, looked at her and smiled. Then he put his arms around her and told her how nice it was to come home and see her in the kitchen. "Just where a woman should be!" he laughed. She punched him in his arm, and he headed off to the bathroom. Stank looked at both of them as if to say, "What about me, can I get something to eat?" Vhannie fed Stank and then checked on the meatloaf before heading into the bathroom. Peoples did not hear her enter the bathroom. He lay in the tub with his eyes closed, lost in the music coming through the headphones in his ears. She sat on the toilet and waited for him to feel her presence. He slowly opened his eyes and began humming along with Al Green's "Simply Beautiful." Vhannie asked him if he wanted company, he said yes and told her to take her clothes off. She did as instructed and stepped into the tub with him.

Jacobs went about his daily activities, never once giving any thought to Levar or any other child. He knew his last grab was done hastily and had probably left him vulnerable. The chance meeting with Peoples left him feeling as though he was being watched. He knew he was taking a chance grabbing a child in the early morning hours, but his desire had gotten the better of him and he thought the inner city would be less of a risk than a middle class suburb. Now he was nervous, he needed to return to a routine. He needed to be a typical suburban dad with a wife and two children. He had to play the part of father, breadwinner, good neighbor and business man. He needed to blend into the fabric of Middle America and pretend he didn't have a predilection for young children. He had to pretend he didn't enjoy the cat-and-mouse game of stalking, kidnapping and molesting children. He had to hide the fact that he liked to keep a reminder of his sick actions by capturing a child's tear in a bottle, where it reminded him of what kind of monster he was. He decided to go about the daily routine of his life's activities until the desire was overwhelming, and then he would do it again.

For now, he went about his day and his night, and never thought about the damage he had done or would continue to do. The next child he grabbed would have to wait.

The next day Peoples decided to make contact with Jeannie to learn what he could about Josey and her stay in Atlanta. He called early that morning and had to leave a message. "Hello, this is Lang Peoples, I got your name from a Google search I did trying to locate Josey Spain. She dated a friend of mine and we're trying to locate her to invite her to a surprise party. If you get a chance, please call me at…" "Hello? Hello, this is Jeannie." The voice on the other end of the phone sounded pleasant, and interested in helping the caller. "Hi, this is Lang, is this Jeannie?" Peoples asked. "Yes, this is Jeannie, how can I be of service?" Peoples made up a story about himself and some friends Josey had known back when she lived in Kansas City who were planning a huge surprise party and wanted to invite her. He asked her if she knew how to get in touch with Josey; was she still living and working there. Jeannie said she had not seen her in two years and the last she'd heard she was back in Kansas City. She told Peoples what she thought Josey was doing and that she was so sorry the two of them had gone their separate ways. She described the life Josey lived before the drugs had taken over. She explained how hurt she had been over her breakup with Huber and how it had taken a toll on her. The pain had severely scarred her and left her feeling wounded and alone. Jeannie talked about how she and Josey met and how after a few months they'd moved in together. She talked about the parties and the drugs and the guilt she felt introducing her to that kind of life, but how everyone else had been able to resist becoming dependent except Josey. It was as if she wanted to become an addict. Peoples listened without speaking a word for fear she would stop and he'd miss something important.

It was as if she needed the drug to be the reason her life changed. Jeannie rambled on about how she changed the story about Huber. At first she'd tell people that he allowed some other preacher to break them up, later after the drugs got her, she told people the break up was due to her addictive personality. If she was addicted to anything, it was to the life she thought they would have together. Josey was as strong as they come, she said, she was never one to back down from anything. "I remember one time when she was on a call for the escort service. She got a trick who wanted her to dress up like a child and pretend he was raping her. The idea so disgusted her, that she got him banned from using the service. "When he found out, he started stalking her. He would sit outside the boutique and wait for her. When she found out, she bought a gun and waited for him to do something so she could blow him away. He found out about her gender reassignment and tried to use that against her; it didn't work because everyone already knew. But the whole thing became too much for her and the drugs became an outlet to help her erase the memories." Peoples sighed, and then asked Jeannie if she remembered the man who stalked Josey. She hesitated for a moment and said she couldn't be sure, but she remembered he was a large white guy and then she said she remembered one more thing about him; "Josey had serviced this guy before the dress-up incident, only that time he asked her to cry for him." Peoples asked her to repeat what she had just said. Jeannie remembered that the first time Josey did a call with the guy, "It was her and another girl and he'd asked Josey to cry for him. It was the strangest thing," Jeannie recalled, "Crying for someone and then capturing their tear on a Q-tip. Who does that?"

she said. Peoples thanked her for the information and said he' try to locate her in Kansas City. After he hung up the phone he felt for the Q-tip in his pocket.

The case of Michael Groves became a cold case for several reasons: other murders had taken its place, Jacobs was a higher priority, and Vhannie had become his once again. Peoples hated to admit he'd dropped the ball, so when she asked him if there had been any news on who killed her husband, he told her he was close to solving it. He never gave any specifics; just that everything he did was getting him closer to the killer. Part of what he said was actually true, although he had said it in haste; he knew that each piece of the puzzle was being assembled to give a face to the person who had killed her husband. Michael, found in that cheap motel room lying atop a lifelike doll, had been murdered and although the autopsy revealed a heart condition, Peoples knew better and he would prove it; just not now. Now he had to find out where Josey was and what she knew, if anything, about the man Vhannie had seen in the bank. He knew the man wasn't Huber's son. Josey and Huber couldn't have produced a child, and he had performed a background check on Huber and found nothing. Huber was as vanilla as they come; before his relationship with Josey, he had been a virgin and anyone who knew him agreed that he had not been a player, unlike Groves.

Huber was what everyone called a "square." When he decided he wanted to become a preacher, it was full steam ahead. He was determined and focused, and did everything by the book. He studied hard, and remained chaste although it was not a requirement for students at the school. There was never any talk about celibacy nor did they enforce it as a rule. Most of the instructors at the school were married with children, but Huber felt it was best to remain free of the thought of sex so that his studies would not suffer. He wanted to understand the plight of Jesus and believed sex caused things to become confused and tangled. He saw the pastor's role as that of biblical disciple. He wanted to be a teacher of the Scripture, not just a preacher of the Word. He often felt that some pastors were in it for the money and, although in the beginning he and Groves thought it was a good 'hustle', he'd soon changed his mind. He felt closer to God as he studied and sought answers. He wanted to make a difference in the lives of others. He never took it for granted when he was made pastor of Greener Pastures over Groves. He also never thought he would meet Josey, but when he did, his life changed.

Josey looked at the man as he took several more pictures; inside she was frightened. When she tried to smile for the photographer, he stopped, and told her to pretend he wasn't there and to act natural. She looked a little confused and just when she thought he would attack her, he handed her the comb. He asked her if she'd like to go into the bathroom and fix her hair before he continued; she said yes. When she returned, he smiled at her and told her to sit on the bed. He looked at her and told her how beautiful she was and how she was so much prettier than the other women he knew. He told her to lie back on the bed and take off her shoes. He walked to the end of the bed and removed them for her and then he smoothed her dress to cover her thighs. He told her that while she was convalescing over the next couple of weeks, he would buy her some new clothes. Kicking her bad habits was going to hard he said, but he was there to help her. He would make sure she was okay and would see to her every need. No more sleeping on the ground or asking gay men she didn't know for food and a place to stay. Josey looked at him and pretended not to be alarmed, but when he mentioned the man who had bought her food and let her spend the night, she was shocked. "How did he know that?" she wondered, but she kept her emotions hidden and displayed a poker face. He told her that from this moment on, the only man in her life was going to be him and he was all she needed. He was going to continue to protect her just as he had planned. He touched her hair and told her to forget all the bad things that had happened to her, because from now on only good things were going to happen, and he would see to it.

Peoples got a call from Jorge asking if he could meet him at the bar. He said he had some information for him about Cindy's murder. He asked him if the new information would net a suspect. Jorge replied yes, and no, but it would be up to Peoples to determine that. He told Jorge he'd be there in about an hour and hung up the phone. Peoples kept his emotions at bay. He'd learned early on that people often had the right intentions when helping the police, but so many times their intentions were self-motivated and lead to nowhere. Jorge seemed to be a nice enough guy and Peoples thought his information was good when he first questioned him, but now he was calling saying he had some new information that might or might not help the case. He wanted to get excited, but he knew better. So he drove to the bar expecting nothing more than conversation and a bunch of half-naked young women. When he walked into the bar, he saw Jorge at a table in the back of the room. The lights were low and the room was dark although it was sunny and bright outside. A young woman, dressed in fishnet hose, short shorts and a bikini top, led him to a table. Jorge ordered Peoples a soda and a shot of bourbon for himself. As Peoples seated himself facing the bar, he stopped him and told him to sit on his side of the table so he could see the stage more clearly. Peoples gave him a puzzled look, but did as he was told.

When the waitress returned with the drinks, Peoples asked Jorge what information he had. Jorge pointed to where a large man, with his back to the two of them, sat a few tables away. The man was drinking and starring at the young woman sliding down the pole. "Him, you see him there, that guy there staring at the girl on stage?" Peoples looked at the man and thought he looked familiar, but he couldn't tell in the dark room as the man's back was to him. "Yeah I see him, but who is he? Is he somebody connected to Cindy's murder?" Peoples asked. "How do you know he's connected, what do you know about him?" Jorge whispered, "That's David Jacobs. You know the guy that owns that building company, real bigwig with the city and all? He was honored not so long ago at some big city thing … you remember, you know who he is, right?" Peoples wanted, but suppressed the urge to walk up to Jacobs, shoot him in his genitals and slit this throat; he smiled at the fantasy. Returning to reality, he said he knew him well enough, but what did he have to do with Cindy's murder. "I don't know if he did," Jorge replied, "but what I do know is that dude is bad news and there's something real nasty about him. I remembered him when he came in today," he continued, "and called you right away because he used to always ask for Cindy whenever he was here. She hated him and called him a creep. One time he asked her to do a lap dance for him and when she refused he called her a whore. She kept her distance from him after that but each night he came in, he'd ask for her anyway. She was kind of scared of him and I remembered that because she had me take her home one night after he propositioned her. Now here's the weird thing, he asked her if she'd cry for him. Ain't that strange? The fucking pervert asked her to cry because he wanted to capture her tears!" Peoples stared at Jacobs, wishing he had super powers and his gaze could cause Jacobs to burst into flames. "Okay, so you think he had something to do with her murder?" he replied to the informant, "If so, I've got to have more than him asking her for a tear. What else do you have?"

Jorge paused for a moment and took a sip of his drink as if the liquid would help his thought process. "I wish I could give you something exact, but I can't. I can only tell you that this guy is real bad. I just know in my gut that this guy had something to do with Cindy's murder! Yeah, I know there's something wrong with that dude. I bet you he's 'el pederasta'!" Peoples knew what he meant and was determined to prove it, but now he needed to prove he was also a murderer and so far he didn't have the proof.

Just then Jacobs got up to leave, dropping a few bills on the table to cover his tab. The dancer who had been on the pole got down from the stage and caught up with him. Peoples couldn't hear their conversation, so he decided to wait to see if the pair would leave together. Jorge, concerned, got up and headed to the bar. He waived the other bartender on and stood pretending to organize bottles as he listened to the two barter over services. Peoples liked Jorge and thought he was doing a good job surveying the pair. He was glad to be able to sit where he was, observing Jacobs without being noticed. That was the thing about a strip club, no one really wanted to be seen buying sexual favors, so bringing attention to oneself or acknowledging anyone else was unusual. The pair continued to haggle; Peoples and Jorge continued to feign disinterest. The young woman seemed surprised at whatever Jacobs whispered in her ear but nodded her head in agreement. Jacobs walked away, and headed outside.

Jorge called the young woman over and asked her what was going on. She just shook her head and said she needed to go make a quick $200.00. The club's policy prohibiting offering additional services outside the club were strict, but no one followed them. Most girls never performed real sexual acts outside the club but most patrons asked for them anyway. No man actually went to a strip club just to watch and get aroused without there being some way to benefit from the excitement. So the men went home to their wives or girlfriends or boyfriends or to a bottle of baby oil and their hand. The girls were there to make a living, to support their families, an education, or a drug habit so they made deals inside the club for services rendered outside the club. As long as Jorge didn't ask the girls didn't tell, and to keep the bar legal, he never asked. This time was different, so he asked the dancer what was going on and what service Jacobs had requested.

Peoples watched, and read Jorge's and the stripper's body language. He remained in his seat, waiting for the pair to leave the club together; then he would follow them. The young woman began gathering her things as she spoke to the manager, complaining that she didn't think it was any of his business what services the man had asked for. She didn't know who Jacobs was and didn't care, all she cared about was the money she was about to make, combined with the $300.00 she had already made; she was done for the day, and it had been a pretty good day at that. Jorge told her to be careful and he'd see her tomorrow. He wiped down the bar and looked over at Peoples who had started to head his way. The stripper went to the door, yelled something to the man waiting for her and headed to the bathroom. Peoples asked Jorge if he knew what the two had discussed. "No, not really," he responded, "I found out early in this place to mind my own business. Even when I ask, they don't really tell me and you know what, I don't think I really want to know. 'A cada uno su propia.' My job is to hire the girls, manage their schedule and make sure they can perform. I think trying to be their father or protector is a little too late and not appreciated, so I mind my own business." Peoples looked at him and smiled. He understood the natural tendency to protect those who society deemed fragile or weak, but he also understood the damage life had done to too many who turned down protection and seemed to seek only an ending. Maybe the highs and lows of life were too unpredictable and unmanageable. Drugs and street life seemed to make sense to some and if it led to the end of things, then so be it. To most of those, life had not been that great to begin with; being born to drug addicted parents, or child abusers, or to those who saw the creation of life as an interruption of their goals and dreams created the pain and suffering so many sought to end. Some eased their pain by hurting themselves or others, especially ones unable to protect themselves like children. Peoples thought about Kayla, Levar and the other children he knew Jacobs had hurt but would never know their names.

He looked at Jorge and saw the humanness in him and wondered why he worked at the club; maybe he didn't really mean it when he said he minds his own business and just possibly this was his way of protecting those who needed it the most. The young woman appeared again and this time she headed out the door.

Peoples asked Jorge where the exit was and if it led to the street. He said yes, and the two men walked quickly to it. Peoples looked out the door and saw the black Explorer head west down Main. He ran to his car and pulled out, following Jacobs and the young woman.

DISCOVERY

Jacobs drove carefully, obeying the speed limit and every traffic light, making sure nothing would prevent him from reaching his destination. Peoples followed him close enough not to lose him but not so close that Jacobs would know he was being followed. The SUV got on the highway and headed toward Kansas. Peoples knew Jacobs lived in Kansas so he wasn't surprised, he figured he was headed somewhere close to his home. But why would he risk doing something close to where he lived? This was strange, he thought. It was just sex, he couldn't understand driving miles to get his rocks off, when a cheap motel had only been blocks away. Maybe the pervert wasn't headed to his house, maybe it wasn't sex he asked the young woman to perform. As he followed Jacobs, his mind was racing and his adrenaline was pumping, he was on overdrive! The SUV continued on; 10, 15 and then 20 miles into Kansas. Peoples relaxed and turned his mind down so that he could think logically. The desire to catch Jacobs was beginning to overwhelm him and he knew that if he didn't calm himself down, he'd mess up. If he caught Jacobs doing something illegal, he'd ruin his chance to arrest him if he wasn't careful. Peoples needed to arrest Jacobs himself so that he could search his house and look for anything to build a solid case against him. What that reason would be, he didn't know just yet, but perhaps it would happen today.

Jacobs exited and drove down several streets until he reached a large building with no windows and one door. Peoples parked up the block and waited for the pair to exit. Jacobs got out first and headed to the door of the building. The stripper waited until Jacobs reappeared and then she got out and went inside. Peoples hesitated for a moment, deciding whether he should go and look around the building or wait until the pair came out. He didn't recognize the building and there were no signs to determine what it was, so he sat and watched a little longer. The street was not a busy one and there were no other cars in the parking lot. Peoples began to imagine what kinds of things were happening in the building and he became restless. It was not like him to be anxious and risk being recognized whenever he was on a stake out. To calm down, he started talking to himself and going over the things he had figured out so far. One: he knew Jacobs was a child molester and he had at least two pieces of evidence he could turn over to forensics to help build a case against him for the kidnapping of Kayla and Levar: two, he found out that Josey was back in KC and had struggled ever since she'd lost Huber: three, there was a man who visited Vhannie's bank that looked like Huber, but couldn't possibly be him: four, there was the small man who was found shot to death in his apartment: five, Cindy the free-spirited stripper, was found murdered in a school parking lot: six, he still didn't know who killed Michael Groves and last but not least, Jacobs and a stripper were fifty feet away from him doing something he was sure was unnatural and yet he couldn't arrest him. Peoples felt like shit; why couldn't he put the pieces together, what was the missing piece? He felt like he'd lost his focus and was being pulled in too many directions. He needed to refocus and try to solve one thing at a time; then and only then would he finally find out who murdered Michael Groves.

He took a deep breath and got out of the car. He walked around the building looking for doors or windows unseen from the front of the building. There were none. He went to the back and found boxes and trash piled together as if someone had been cleaning. He scanned the trash and found a box that had a name on it. 'Green BioChemicals.' Peoples wasn't sure why, but he felt compelled to keep it. He continued to look through the trash for anything that could connect Jacobs with child kidnapping and molestation. He was about to pick up another box, when he heard voices, "Stop, stop it, you pervert!" Peoples was sure it was the voice of the young woman who had accompanied Jacobs. He pressed himself against the side of the building and inched slowly toward the voices. "Look, you little slut, I paid you and I want what I paid for," a man's voice said, "you either do it on your own, or I'll give you a reason to give it to me." Peoples moved slowly and cautiously toward the two making sure he was not seen or heard. He had traveled almost to the front of the building, staying against the wall so that Jacobs wouldn't notice him. Jacobs and the girl continued to argue as Peoples stayed quiet, listening for anything he could use to make a case against Jacobs. He half-hoped something would happen so he'd have an excuse to knock Jacobs to the ground, handcuff him and wait for assistance to take him to jail. Just then the two went back inside the building. Peoples took a deep breath and headed to his car. When he got in, he looked in the glove compartment and pulled out a GPS tracking device. He knew it was against precinct policy to tag a car without a warrant, but this was different, he told himself, and he was going to do it anyway. He moved quickly back to the parking lot and placed the tracking device underneath the truck. He had just made his way back to his car, when the couple exited the building and got in the truck.

Peoples sat and watched the two, noticing how quiet the woman had become. Her appearance gave no hint of what occurred in the building and she didn't appear to have been injured, so he did nothing. The SUV pulled out of the parking lot and headed east back to Kansas City; Peoples followed. As they sped past him he was unable to see inside the tinted windows to determine if anything was happening that would allow him to pull them over. He hoped to catch Jacobs hitting the girl or notice a torn dress, black eye, bruises on her body, anything that Jacobs could have been arrested for. Whatever he paid for he got, so the two were now headed back to where they started, only this time Peoples would be able to track him and the next time Jacobs headed to the inner city or suburb to steal an innocent child, he wouldn't get away.

Peoples returned to the police station and took the box from the building with him. The name on the box was clearly from some type of chemical company but what types of chemicals he wasn't sure, so he decided to use the available police resources to find out. He ran the name through a database and found that the company was based out of India and manufactured perfumes. He was surprised at that, and wondered what Jacobs needed with a company that made fragrances. He knew Jacobs was known for designing and building, so he couldn't see the connection a designer and builder would have with a chemical company who produced perfumes. He decided he should keep the box and the information he had just discovered and wait until he had more to make any sense of it.

Across town the couple in the apartment spent their days talking and eating and their nights as if they didn't know each other. Josey was no longer fearful of her benefactor; she was too busy going through withdrawal since she had been unable to get drugs. The young man rarely left her side. When he did, it was only to get the bare necessities. They ate sparingly, mainly vegetables and soup. He told her it was to get her healthy and the fewer chemicals she put in her system, the easier it would be for her to get clean. He allowed her to drink only water, and when she begged for a cup of tea he ignored her. He insisted that she bathe twice a day, every day, and put olive oil on her body, including her hair. He told her that her life had been full of toxins and evil spirits and now it was time to cleanse not only her body, but her mind as well. Each night after her bath, he read the Bible to her.

The days turned into weeks without a peep from Jacobs. Peoples was concerned that the tracking device wasn't working, so he decided to pay a visit to the Jacobs house. As he parked several houses down, he noticed Jacobs getting into his wife's Honda. "Shit, he thought, so you've been driving you're wife's car, you pervert." He watched Jacobs pull away from the house and noticed the tracking device was idle. The truck must be in the garage he thought, so he decided to follow the Honda. Jacobs drove several minutes until he arrived at the onramp to the highway. Peoples followed; sure he had not been noticed. After passing several exits, Peoples realized Jacobs was headed back to the non-descript building where he had taken the stripper. The car slowed at the exit where the building appeared and both men turned off. Jacobs pulled into the parking lot and got out of his car. Peoples parked across the street to get a better view and waited to see what he was up to. When Jacobs went around the back of the building instead of going inside, Peoples began to wonder if he was there because of the trash in the back. He remembered the box he had taken back to the station had come from a chemical company. He wondered if Jacobs had mistakenly put the box in the trash and if so, why? Why was that box important? It didn't make sense that he would have dealings with a company that produced fragrances: his primary business was designing and constructing professional buildings, so a chemical company that produced perfumes just didn't make sense. He continued to watch as Jacobs reappeared, looking confused and agitated. He paced around the Honda and then stood, with his hands on his hips, lost in thought. Peoples smiled as he watched Jacobs get in the Honda and head back the way he had come.

Peoples followed Jacobs back to Kansas City. Jacobs wondered aloud as he drove. "What did I do with that damn box?" he muttered. "It's got to be there, where else could it be? I need to retrace my steps. I need to remember where that box is, I can't afford to have stuff like that lying around any and everywhere. It's got to be there, maybe I should turn around…I must have overlooked it". Jacobs continued talking to himself, expecting the answer to come to him, but after several miles he realized he had made it back home without the box. Peoples followed the car and could see the man talking to himself. He wondered what Jacobs was saying; he figured it had to be about the trash, more specifically the missing box. Jacobs pulled into his driveway and raised the garage door. The black Explorer was sitting there, quietly waiting for the next child abduction. He pulled the Honda into the garage and closed the door. Peoples waited and watched to see if the Explorer was coming out; it never did. He waited a few more minutes, hoping Jacobs would emerge and attempt to grab another innocent child. He actually *wanted* him to do it; *needed* him to, so that he could be done watching him pretending he was a regular guy, when in reality he was scum. The sound of his phone buzzing brought him back to reality. He answered it and heard Vhannie's voice on the other end.

She told him she was headed home and asked if he needed her to do anything before she left. He had several loads of laundry that hadn't been folded and she would fold it if he wanted her to. He said no, but wanted her to stay for a while longer since he was headed that way. He wanted her opinion about something so she should hang around. Vhannie agreed and hung up the phone.

Jacobs went into his secret room and looked around for the missing box. He was sure it had to be there since it wasn't at the building. He normally kept all the boxes from Green BioChemicals in his room. His normal routine was to burn them after emptying the contents. He was always very careful, that was the reason he had never been caught, not even questioned. His bottles now totaled 90, just 10 more to go and he was on his way to launching his new business. But the box was nowhere to be found and he became agitated. He started throwing things around and pacing back and forth trying to recall why the box wasn't where it should be. This was not good he thought why was the box at his other building in the first place. He was getting nervous and knew he had to find it.

Then he remembered the small man who had tracked him down at the mayor's ceremony. He remembered the man approaching him and how he had made him feel even smaller than he physically was by ignoring him. He remembered the conversations he'd had with the man and how a shot through a peep hole had put an end to him. Then he remembered another phone call and how the person on the other end was going to take the small man's place. None of that meant anything to him now, the only thing that mattered now was finding the box and he didn't have a clue where to start. He went to his case and pulled out a bottle that reminded him of one of his first grabs. It was a powerful scent, mixed with the smells of garlic and onions. He closed his eyes and went back to the little boy who begged outside a pizza restaurant. He remembered his beautiful round face and his soiled clothes. He touched the bottle to his cheek. He recalled the little boy's face as the tears flowed when he took his innocence away and put it in the bottle.

PROTECTOR AND INVESTIGATOR

Josey and her Protector continued their patient/caretaker relationship. He bathed her and washed her hair. He bought her new clothes and gave her medicine. She told him about the life she lived before Huber and after he was gone. She shared her dreams with him and allowed him to offer her hope and solitude as the desire for the drugs left her body. She thought he was different than anyone she had known and wondered why he rescued her. He appeared caring and attentive at times, and other times he was nervous and distracted, especially when he was on the phone. She wondered about the person on the other end of the line, and why the conversations between them left him angry and irritated. Once, after a conversation, he left the apartment and was gone for several hours. When he returned, he looked as if he had been in a fight. His clothes were disheveled and he had scratch marks on his arms and hands. Josey wanted to ask what happened, but the look on his face and the way he paced back and forth told her to remain quiet. He had a bag in his hand and began to rifle through it looking for something, frowning.

She got up and went into the bathroom. When she returned, he appeared calmer. She sat on the sofa as he stared at her with the bag in his hand. He told her that he was trying to take care of some business that had gone on far too long. He was the only one, he said, who could take care of it; just like he was the only one who could take care of her. It was his job, his fate and his mission to handle things no one else could. She smiled at her Protector and asked if he was hungry. She wanted to change subjects and she hoped making dinner would calm the situation. He asked her if she wanted to cook, because cooking was his job. She nodded yes, and proceeded into the kitchen.

The atmosphere in the apartment changed, both patient and Protector settled down and soon the delicious odor of food was in the air. Josey knew that soon she'd have to find a way out. She was happy he had rescued her, and even happier he helped her kick her drug habit, but it had been over two weeks since the pair had been together in the small apartment and she was getting restless. After dinner, the man went in to take a shower and returned to lie down on the bed. He told Josey she should lie down with him, and patted the bed. She did as she was told as he put his arms around her and laid his head on her breast. He was asleep in less than twenty minutes as she lay looking at the ceiling, planning her escape.

Peoples arrived home and was greeted by his faithful, four-legged friend. Stank looked up at his master as Peoples scratched behind his ears and patted him on the head; then he trotted into the kitchen where Vhannie was making a drink. Peoples kissed her on the cheek and took the drink as he sat on the stool at the island. She made another drink and sat across from him, waiting for him to wind down. He smiled at her and began describing the day's events. He told her about his conversation with the stripper and following Jacobs. He told her how he followed Jacobs back to his house and waited, wishing that he'd come out and go searching for another child so that he could arrest him. He explained that he had been going off in so many directions since Michael's murder that he was sure he was on to something but couldn't quite put his hands on it. He looked at her and scratched his head as he told her about the dead girl whose parents described her as a disappointment because she danced for a living. He told her that he knew Josey was in town, but he hadn't had a chance to locate her. He got up from the table, grabbed the bottle of cognac and filled his glass.

Vhannie listened attentively without interrupting. He drained the glass and filled it again. Then he walked over to her and pulled her up from the stool. He kissed her hard and ran his hands all over her body, as if searching for something. He kissed her neck and then her breast as she tried to understand what was happening, not wanting him to stop. He turned her around and pushed her over the island as he pulled her pants down. He stood back and looked at her. She could hear him removing his pants, and then he was inside her. He pushed deep and hard as she tried to steady herself, grabbing her hips, moving her back and forth to meet his thrust. Neither made a sound, acting in a primal way that seemed right for the moment. Then, a grunt, a soft cry, and she knew it was over. He fell on her and kissed the back of her neck, saying he was sorry. She said nothing as she straightened her clothes and pulled her pants back on. Peoples gathered his clothes and retreated to his study.

Vhannie went into the bathroom and cleaned up, then to the study where he sat staring at the label he had found from Jacobs' building with the name of the chemical manufacturer on it. She took it from him, and asked what it was. Peoples told her that it was on a box in the trash behind the building where Jacobs had taken the stripper, saying that at the time he didn't know what it meant. He had since discovered the location of the company and what they manufactured. What he didn't know was why Jacobs did business with them. Vhannie asked him to move over, and sat down at the computer. She began typing in the name of the company and searched for other manufacturers of fragrances. Dozens of companies came up, all similar to Green Bio-Chemicals. Most were headquartered in India and China. She wondered if the fact that they were outside the US had anything to do with anything. She went to the manufacturers' home pages, seeking the nature of the business and the name of companies they did business with. Jacobs' business was not listed, which seemed odd, but not surprising since what he did for a living had nothing to do with the making of fragrances. Peoples watched as she typed, read, and typed again. He smiled, thanking his lucky stars she had given him another chance; he was determined not to mess up again.

She continued her search and jotted down the names of some of the companies listed. Some companies posted a link to their websites, which allowed her to see what their main business was. After viewing several, she went back to Green Bio-Chemicals and wrote down some numbers. Peoples watched her work the keyboard, hoping with each stroke that something of value would emerge. He got up, and came back with the bag containing the cotton swab he had gotten from Levar and the receipt from DQ he'd found in Jacob's driveway. Vhannie continued her investigation, typing and cross-referencing the list of companies found on the web page of the fragrance company.

Then she stopped, as something she read made her pause. Peoples noticed her hesitation and asked, "What's happening?" She told him to come and read something she had stumbled upon. On one page of the company's website was listed numerous products the company manufactured. Perfumes were just one part of what the company produced; it also offered other chemicals, in addition to services as a manufacturer of oils essential to the production of perfumes. In other words, it was also a company that offered private-label services for those interested in producing their own line of fragrances. Vhannie looked at him and asked if he thought it meant anything. Peoples looked at the website and then he looked at her and shook his head. "No, I just don't see why or how it connects to anything. I mean Jacobs is a bastard who builds large buildings and likes to grab innocent children. I don't see the connection with a company who makes perfumes. I mean, he doesn't sell perfumes; he's just a son of a bitch."

Vhannie looked at the screen again and then she asked Peoples what he had in his bag. He pulled out the receipt and told her how he retrieved it one night after watching Jacobs' house. He explained to her that he had Jacobs under surveillance and, after Kayla's abduction; he found the receipt in Jacobs' driveway. He hadn't thought much of it then, he explained, until he met with Kayla and her mother and the little girl told how Jacobs bought ice cream for her. So he kept the receipt and went to DQ hoping to see video of the Explorer coming through the drive-thru on the night of the abduction. As luck would have it, he said, they didn't have any video and the cashier didn't remember a large man in a black Explorer with a small child. He'd kept the receipt anyway. Then he stopped, and looked at the Q-Tip. Vhannie noticed the hesitation and asked him what else did he have? He stood up and began to walk back and forth across the room; hoping the movement would help him think more clearly. Before he showed her the Q-Tip he asked her to do a quick search for the ingredients found in the manufacturing of perfumes. Vhannie did a search and started quoting the ingredients; oils, alcohol, plant sources, other chemicals, etc. "Why?" she asked. Peoples pulled at his chin and scratched his head. Something is there, he thought. The he recalled a conversation he had with Jeanne about Josey. He pulled out the Q-Tip Levar had given him and walked over to Vhannie.

"What if I told you there's a connection with the chemical company, Jacobs, and this Q-Tip?" She looked puzzled, and then smiled as she realized he knew something he hadn't told her yet. "Well, I would say, 'what else do you have?'" Peoples walked out of the room and came back with a book in his hand. "Hold on a minute," he said, "this is a biochemistry textbook I've had for years, and I think the there's a common ingredient to be found." He flipped through several pages and then he read aloud the chemicals in human tears. "Here," he said, "tears contain some oil, water and mucus. It also states that tears from women tend to lower testosterone in men."

Vhannie looked puzzled, and waited for him to put the pieces together and make sense. "Baby, follow me with this," he said, "tears contain oil, perfumes contain oil, and tears from women can lower testosterone in men. What if Jacobs is trying to make a perfume?" She looked at him as if he were speaking a foreign language. "I don't follow you," she said. "Okay, I guess I left out a huge piece of this puzzle. When I spoke to Jeanne about Josey, she told me about an incident where Josey had a date with a john who wanted her to cry so that he could capture her tears on a Q-Tip. Levar gave me this," Peoples said, holding up the Q-Tip from the bag, "after he was abducted by Jacobs, and told me that, when he cried, Jacobs touched his face with a Q-Tip to capture his tear. Vhannie looked confused and disgusted. The thought of what Jacobs had done to Levar to make him cry, and to collect his tears was even more disturbing.

"So, what I'm thinking is, this pervert is trying to invent some type of perfume, and by collecting tears from women, he can use it to control his urge to molest children." Vhannie looked surprised at the information Peoples had collected. She knew he was assigned neither Kayla's nor Levar's case. She knew he had spoken to Jeanne, but she didn't know what the conversation had been about. Now she was hearing for the first time that he had a Q-Tip from Levar that was taken from Jacobs' house or some other place he'd taken the child. She thought about Josey's john asking for her tears and tried to see the connection Peoples saw. Peoples looked at her and invited her to sit down while he went over the things he knew and why he thought he finally knew what was going on. "Okay, think about this for a moment: Jacobs is a child molester and for several months I have watched and waited for him to make a move. He has been pretty careful and not made any mistakes. He grabs little Kayla and takes her to get ice cream after he does whatever he does to her. She kind-of remembers him and she kind-of doesn't, but she does remember he took her to get ice cream because she was a 'good girl' after he molested her. He grabs Levar and, unbeknownst to him, the boy finds a Q-Tip and puts it in his pocket. Levar tells me about the crying and that Jacobs touched his cheek to get a tear. I talked to Jeanne about Josey and discovered that when she was turning tricks, she met a john who paid her to cry and captured her tear on a Q-Tip. I know it all sounds confusing and crazy, but my gut tells me it's all relative." Vhannie tried to take it all in and make it make sense in her mind, but the pieces didn't all fit together for her. She looked at Peoples and asked a question: "What does this have to do with the stripper, and what does this have to do with Michael's murder?" People's sighed and then said, "I'm not sure yet, maybe something, maybe nothing." At that moment, his phone started to buzz and he realized the pervert was on the move. The GPS tracking on the Explorer was activated.

Jacobs tried to suppress his desire to molest another child, especially since his last kidnapping was done in haste. He knew he was bound to make a mistake if he wasn't careful, but the last couple of days had not quenched his desire. He thought the fling with the young stripper would have been enough to stop the whisper in his head from getting louder and the desire in his groin from growing, but it didn't and he found himself in his safe room, reliving his very first grab. The fragrance from his first take, though, sent his desire into overdrive. He needed to satisfy his demons and he was too close to completing his inventory of one hundred bottles. He got into the Explorer and headed out to find a child. As he drove through neighborhood after neighborhood he began to think he should abandon his mission. The tree-lined streets were quiet, and absent of the sounds of small children. Jacobs continued to look for his prey.

Peoples was startled when his phone alerted him that the object of his obsession was on the move. He kissed Vhannie and bolted from the house, never saying a word as he drove away. His house was only a few miles away from the area Jacobs was driving in, and his adrenaline pumped as he pursued his prey. Soon, he was on Jacobs' tail, making sure he was not detected. The two men drove on; one hunting for children, the other hunting for justice. Jacobs slowed as he saw two children walking toward a house, being as cautious as possible as he watched them make their way to the house. Two, he thought, and smiled as the idea of grabbing more than one child made him shudder with excitement. If he grabbed two each time he went out, he'd get to one hundred bottles that much faster. But he quickly dismissed the idea as soon as it had entered his mind. He knew better, two kids were not better than one; it would be harder to keep them quiet, to keep them from remembering. So far, he had been able to keep doing what he did because alone, children were easy to distract and frighten. He knew how to convince them to keep their mouths shut when he dropped them off, but he knew that in numbers everyone was stronger, even children. He watched them anyway, as the thought of what he would do got him excited. He pulled the truck to the opposite side of the street, and watched the children go into the house. As he did, he noticed others arriving and realized they were going to a party.

He had hit pay dirt. So many children meant someone was bound to allow their child to walk home alone. Parents were so predictable, he thought, allowing their most precious commodity to go unprotected. He knew some parents did it to allow their children the ability to grow up without constant supervision, but it almost always caused problems. Tonight, he hoped some parent's misstep would be his fortune. Peoples watched Jacobs survey the children going in and out of the house. He figured there was a party happening in the house. Birthday, perhaps, he thought as he waited for the pervert to act. Jacobs did nothing, stalking his prey. The children, most between ages eight and twelve, ran in and out, and more continued to arrive. Peoples thought the number of children had now reached about twenty from the time he had arrived.

Each child arrived with a gift, except for one little boy who seemed to be out of place. Most of the kids were nicely dressed, in designer jeans and polo shirts. The girls were all dressed in the latest fashions, including some in high heels. Peoples shook his head at that, thanking God he didn't have any kids, especially girls. As he looked at the little girls he remembered the time Vhannie told him she was pregnant and the stupid way he'd reacted. He often wondered if his life would have been different if he had been more mature. He was just thankful she was.

Jacobs was like a lion in the jungle; stealthy and quiet as he waited for the most vulnerable to show him- or herself. The children enjoyed the party, at times spilling out onto the front porch, cups in hand and laughter abounding. The parents of the birthday child appeared outside and asked the kids to come back in because it was time to open the gifts. The little boy who was different from the rest appeared again, and stayed on the porch as the others went inside. He looked around the yard and down at his clothes, realizing he was out of place. He sat on the steps of the house and waited for the unwrapping of presents to end. The father of the birthday child noticed the little boy on the steps and asked him to come back inside. The little boy looked up at him, and said he would rather wait because he hadn't brought a gift and felt bad. The father told him that it was okay and he should come inside anyway. The little boy stood up to go in when another boy came out the door. He looked at the outcast and began to belittle him for not being able to afford a gift. Then three more kids appeared and they joined in chastising the outcast child. He began to cry, and walked away from the party. Jacobs started his truck to follow his prey. He was ready to pounce.

The little boy walked slowly at first and then started to run. He cried as he ran, oblivious to the black truck following him. Peoples stayed back as he watched Jacobs stalk his prey. He waited, and grew angrier as he thought about what Jacobs intended to do if he got the little boy in his truck. His insides were turning red-hot as he watched the pervert in action. Jacobs continued to follow the child, waiting for the right moment when he would catch his next victim. The little boy slowed down as he approached a small house with an old, beat-up truck in the driveway. Jacobs pulled over to the side and realized the boy had arrived home. He looked around the neighborhood to see if there were any adults around, never noticing the car that had been following him the entire time. The little boy had almost made it to his door when Jacobs rolled down his window and called out to him. Peoples put his hand on his gun, his heart racing. The little boy looked startled as he heard the man in the truck calling out to him. Jacobs called out again, and asked the boy if he could give him directions. The boy hesitated and remained in his yard, staring at the man in the truck. Jacobs told him that his navigation system wasn't working, and he needed to get somewhere. He asked the boy if he knew how to get to Hawser Street. The boy shook his head no and started to go into his house. Jacobs asked him if he could come over to the truck and help him draw a map of where he was and then he would be able to find his way. The boy said no, and went inside.

Jacobs was furious as he watched his prey walk away from him. He began yelling inside his truck, pulling his own hair. Peoples watched him, laughing at the failed attempt. Then he got mad and decided to call in the Explorer's plates. He wanted a reason to arrest him and lock him away, if for no other reason than to get him off the street for one night. His wishes were answered when the plates came back expired. He called a friend he knew who patrolled the area and told him about a black Explorer he'd noticed speeding through a neighborhood. Peoples told him he was on his way to a meeting and had been driving by when he noticed the speeding truck. He didn't want the patrolman to know he had been watching Jacobs, but he wanted him off the street. The officer thanked him and said he'd be right there.

The patrol car arrived just as Jacobs began driving away. He saw the flashing lights behind him and wondered why he was being pulled over. When the officer approached his vehicle and asked for his documentation, he looked surprised. He produced his license but couldn't find his insurance card. The officer told him that his plates were expired and that he was going to have to ask him to step out of the car. Peoples, waiting, watched it all unfold from a block away and grinned as he saw Jacobs being escorted to the patrol car. About thirty minutes later, he saw a tow truck arrive and place the Explorer on the bed of the truck to be hauled away. "Excellent!" he thought, never expecting tonight's events would put the predator behind bars, if only for a few hours. He decided to take a trip to the bar and talk to the stripper Jacobs had taken to the windowless building.

Peoples arrived at the bar and greeted Jorge with a big handshake and a smile. He asked about the stripper and if she happened to be working today. Jorge pointed to the stage and said she'd be done in about 10 minutes. He offered Peoples a cup of coffee as he waited. This time Peoples turned down the coffee in favor of cognac. He wasn't on duty, and after tonight's arrest he needed a celebration drink. The dancer finished her show, and headed for the bar. Jorge introduced her to Peoples, saying he was a friend of Cindy's and wanted to ask her a couple of questions. Peoples asked her if they could sit down for a minute, she could get her off her feet and he wouldn't take up much of her time. The young woman sat down, looked at Peoples, and folded her arms as if to imply she was not going to cooperate. Peoples asked her about the guy she left with a few days ago. She looked at him and said, "I know you, you ain't a friend of Cindy's, you're a policeman. You're that cop that came by here a few days after Cindy was found killed. Don't you remember me? I'm Cindy's ex's new girlfriend, remember?" Peoples looked closely at her and it all came back to him. "Yes, I remember you, I didn't, but now I do. So can you help me or not?" She looked him up and down and then said, "Yes, I'll try."

"The guy you left with the other day, he was tall, large guy, drove a back Explorer, where did he take you?" She sighed, and said they went to a building where he kept boxes and stuff. "He took me to this place and wanted to do it in a room where he's got a bunch of bottles and flasks and all kinds of stuff like a chemistry lab. I mean it's got tables with stoves and burners and things you'd find in a medical building. There were these cabinets with drawers and stuff locked in them. It was full of stuff and it smelled funny." Peoples asked her to describe the smell. "You know, like flowers and stuff. I don't know, like maybe he was growing some rare flowers or plants or stuff." Peoples looked at her and asked if they had sex.

"Yeah, we did it, I mean he just wanted a blow job, but then he asked me to do something real weird." "Weird, what's weird?" Peoples asked. "He asked me to cry, just like that, this fucking pervert wanted me to cry for him." "Did you?" Peoples asked. She looked strangely at the detective and said, softly, "Yes." Peoples leaned toward her and asked her again. "Yes! Yes," she said. "I cried for him, but not because I wanted to! He said if I didn't he'd give me something to cry for! I was scared. I thought I was going to wind up like Cindy." Peoples looked confused and startled at the young woman's comment. "Why would you think you'd wind up like Cindy, what do you know about Cindy's murder?

The young woman excused herself to go to the bathroom and when she returned she had a drink in her hand. "About six months ago Cindy started dating this little guy who used to come in here with the pervert. I never paid them much attention until one day when Cindy started yelling at the big guy. Apparently he asked her for lap dance and she said no. The guy was so obnoxious that Cindy poured a drink on him and walked away. I followed her into the dressing room to find out what happened. She told me he asked her to cry for him. I said so, so what's wrong with that? She told me he said he wanted to keep her tears in a bottle so that whenever he wanted to remember her, he'd pull out the bottle that held her tears." Peoples looked at Cindy's friend, not wanting to give anything away, but inside he was jumping for joy. It was just as he had thought; the pervert was capturing tears to keep as a memento. Most serial killers keep items to remind them of the kill and Jacobs was keeping tears. The disgusting bastard! Just as he rejoiced inside he knew he was nowhere near arresting him for good. Something was missing in the story about capturing tears.

Human tears placed in a bottle for keeps didn't make sense. Tears were made of water and were odorless; it didn't add up. There was something else going on in Jacobs head and Peoples was getting close to finding out.

The young woman continued to talk about Cindy and how the she and the small man began dating. "It was weird, the two of them," she said, "he was a small man with average looks, nothing worth noting about him, and she was beautiful and a real sweet person. I used to ask her what she saw in him and she'd say he had the most beautiful heart she'd ever seen. I never saw that in him, but then again I never really knew him. One day he was here all the time and the next thing you know he was gone. I think he was shot in the head or something at his house." Peoples listened as the woman talked, sharing all she knew. "Oh, I remember now, I think he got shot in the shower," she said "Yeah, that's it! Cindy said he was shot through the door while he was getting out of the shower." Peoples excused himself, and almost ran to his car.

TURNING THE TABLE

At the police station, people were anxiously waiting to be heard so they could get their car from the city impound lot. Jacobs was standing as he waited for his wife to bring the insurance information and money to pay his ticket. He was angry for several reasons: getting a ticket for expired plates but most importantly for missing out on a grab. He was sure he was going to grab a child and satisfy his unnatural desires. He was confident he would be able to add to his collection of "Innoscents." Instead, he found himself in a police station waiting for his wife to bail him out. The thought of explaining why and where he was, was starting to make him angry. He had been careful and before he attempted to call out to the boy, he'd looked around and never noticed the police car. So when he saw the flashing lights, he was surprised. He thought he was getting more and more careless. There was something happening around him causing him to take more chances and he needed to slow things down, or the next time he went to jail it would be for keeps.

Élan arrived, and paid the violation. She never said a word to Jacobs as they drove to the lot to get his truck. The children were secured in the back of the Honda. Jacobs and Élan barely looked at each other. He got out of the car and headed to his truck. A young man in his twenties appeared out of nowhere as he made his way to the Explorer. "Hey! Hey, you gonna need these," he said, and held the keys in the air as Jacobs reached for them. "Don't fuck with me, he told the lot kid, just give me my goddamn keys so I can get the fuck out of here." The young man smiled, showing a full set of rotten teeth, and handed the keys to Jacobs. "Don't get all worked up man, I held your keys for you to show you something. Jacobs didn't want to talk to the kid and didn't care what he had to say. He snatched the keys and unlocked the door. As he climbed in the truck, the kid held up a small device and said, "You might want to keep this, I found it underneath your car." Jacobs looked at the device, and asked him what it was. "It's a GPS tracking device, asshole."

He grabbed it from the kid and asked him where he found it. He got out of the truck and followed the kid toward the back of the truck. "Right here, underneath the passenger rear wheel," the kid said, "Guess your old woman don't trust you, huh?" The kid laughed. Jacobs knew Élan hadn't put the tracking device on his truck. He knew she didn't care where he went or what he did as long he didn't bother her. She was annoyed that she had to bail him out of jail which was why she never said a word to him inside the jail or on their way to the lot. The love in their marriage had been lost a long time ago, even before he started grabbing children. No, it wasn't Élan, but who it could be, he couldn't be sure. He reached in his glove compartment and pulled out a small locked case. He pulled out a hundred-dollar bill and handed it to the lot kid. Then he drove away.

Peoples drove to his house as if it were on fire. He pulled into the driveway, and burst through the door. Vhannie and Stank lay on the sofa looking at a court show. He grabbed the remote and turned the television off. She sat up, asking, "What, what is it?" "Vhannie, come with me I have to show you something." She followed him into the study where the Q-Tip, receipt and box label lay on the desk beside the computer. "I spoke with the stripper who left with Jacobs the day I found the box label. Here's what she told me: he tried to get Cindy to cry for him so that he could put her tears in a bottle and keep them. He also made this girl cry and captured some of her tears. He told Cindy that whenever he wanted to remember her, all he had to do was pull out the bottle that held her tears." Vhannie looked intrigued but not quite sure of where he was going with the information he had. "Think about it, he's capturing tears and putting them in bottles." Vhannie looked at the Q-Tip and the label from chemical company. "I think I know the role of the chemical company," she said. "What?" Peoples asked. She looked at the label and the list of ingredients used to make perfumes. "He's buying all kinds of scents and other chemicals needed to make perfume and adding the tears of his victims. He adds scents like flowers or trees or other things that remind him of his victims and then he adds their tears to make a memory of the event." Peoples looked shocked and happy at the same time. "The tears are merely symbolic of the event, but the oils he buys from Green Bio-Chemical are specific to the environment he captures his victim in. Peoples recited the idea again and again as Vhannie's conclusion set in. "Tomorrow I'm going to call the company to find out what kinds of fragrances he orders." "No, you're not," Vhannie said, "I'll call. You need to find out what this has to do with Michael's murder.

Jacobs drove to his building and pulled into the parking lot, as he got out he looked around expecting to see a police car on his tail; there was no one there. He hurried inside and went to the room where made his "Innoscents". He looked around at the boxes of scents he'd ordered and inspected the labels on each one making sure they were firmly attached. Nothing seemed out of place and everything he'd ordered was accounted for. He looked inside the drawer of a cabinet that contained a number of oils representing everything from trees to flowers to the ocean. It was all accounted for. Then he opened another cabinet and pulled out two bottles. These contained Cindy's and the other dancer's tears. He had not found time to complete the strippers' perfumes so that he could take them home to his safe room, so they sat while he tried to grab another child. Tonight he would take them with him and place them in his cabinet in the safe room so that whenever he wanted to remember them they would only be a few feet away.

He got back in the truck and headed to his house. As he drove he tried to think of someone who would put a tracking device on his car. He didn't really have any enemies that he knew of. His unnatural desires kept him secluded most of the time, so he barely socialized with anyone. The business kept him busy when he wasn't tracking little children and the last time he was out and about was the ceremony with the Mayor. He couldn't think of a soul that needed to know his whereabouts. Then he remembered the phone call from the man in the apartment letting him know that things were not over and that he was going to get what he deserved. He didn't know who the man was, the only one who had ever threatened him before was shot through the peep hole of his apartment. He thought he was done tidying up loose ends.

Josey realized that to plan her escape would not be easy. Her protector rarely left the apartment, except to get food or things he deemed necessary. He was very frugal, never buying name brand items; her clothes although stylish, came from thrift stores. She noticed he liked to buy clothes that had designer tags in them, although they had the scent of a thrift store. She knew the scent well from her days before moving to Kansas City. When she lived in St Louis, her lover always monitored the money she spent. If she shopped at a well-known department store, regardless of the price, he thought it cost too much. So she learned how to navigate her way through thrift stores, finding the best out of the worst she saw. The food he bought was store-brand, never brand-name. Josey thought he was either very cheap, or very eccentric. There was something about him that made her uneasy. She decided the next time he left, she'd follow. She took note of his lengthier disappearances, and decided she would make her getaway during those times.

She watched as he showered, shaved and put on a clean shirt, paired with black trousers. Then he grabbed his briefcase and told her he would be back shortly. After the door closed, she looked around the apartment searching for any and everything that belonged to her. There wasn't much to get since he'd found her on the street. After he rescued her, he'd bought her several dresses, cosmetics, underwear and 2 pairs of shoes; she quickly gathered them and threw them in a plastic grocery bag. She looked around the apartment for something of his, thinking it was important. Why she didn't know; she just knew she should. It was a strange feeling, but she didn't let that deter her from looking for something to identify him. She looked on the floor, then underneath the bed, where she saw a picture. It was an old Polaroid of a family. As she looked at the photograph, she thought she recognized him, but she couldn't be sure. She decided to keep it, and put it in her purse. Once packed, she looked out the window, making sure he was not nearby, or returning to the apartment. When she was sure he was not able to stop her, she left, closing the door behind her.

Jacobs arrived home and went immediately to his safe room. He pulled out the bottles containing the stripper's tears and placed them in his case. He was still concerned over finding the GPS tracking on his truck, but thought now was not the time to focus on it. He had bigger things to deal with and the first order of business was to do another grab. He was furious when his last attempt had been foiled by the police. Although the little boy had gone inside, he wanted to wait for another child to walk home alone and then he would have gotten what he came out for. Instead he got a $200.00 ticket and an angry wife who hated his guts but had to bail him out of jail. He also found out that someone had been tracking his every move. As he sat down in his big chair he leaned his head back, trying to figure out who could have gotten that close to him. He pulled the tracking device out of his pocket and began inspecting it. He noticed a serial number on the back side and wrote it down. He turned on the PC, and began typing in a description and serial number of the device. The GPS tracker was sold online for anybody to purchase. What he needed was someone smarter than he, who would be able to track down the person responsible for placing it on his car. He decided to pay his tech guy a visit.

Before leaving he decided to pull out one of his first fragrances. The bottle was older and larger than the newer ones. It was from one of his first grabs, when he was just starting the process. As he grabbed more children and found Green BioChemicals his process became streamlined and the newer bottles looked very professional. The very fact that it was one of his very first grabs, held a special place in his distorted mind. He opened the bottle and held it to his nose. The memories came flooding back as if they were brand new, yet it happened over twenty years ago. The day and time remained fresh in his mind. The smell of fresh cut grass and morning dew from a warm Sunday morning. He remembered driving slowly that day, not really thinking anything or wanting anyone, but there she was; this pretty, small, brown little girl with a round face playing innocently by herself. She had several dolls seated at a table with a flowered table cloth and play dishes. She was the gracious hostess of a lively party as she passed around pretend coffee to each of her guests. Jacobs noticed her, she was so beautifully innocent that he wanted to hold her and smell her. He smiled as he watched her, thinking she was the smell of everything new, fresh and good. Like morning dew, she was created by God and he wanted to remember that smell forever. He walked up to her and started talking. A man came around from the back of the house and noticed Jacobs. He nodded to him and smiled as he went back to his yard work. Jacobs took the child's hand, and she followed him to his car. He left with her and after several hours of capturing her tears he returned her to her home, innocence lost, preserved in a bottle kept by a perverted man who would continue to pursue his strange desire for years to come. Neither the child nor her father ever recovered from the incident and she became a damaged soul. Jacobs inhaled deeply, remembering the first grab and the first tears lost. He smiled remembering the small child and placed the bottle back in the case. Then he left the room and headed out to find out what he could about the tracking device.

As he drove to meet his tech friend, he stopped at a red light, and then noticed a car next to him that he recognized. He wasn't sure where he had seen the car or the driver in it, but he knew it was one he had seen before. As the light turned green it hit him; it was the police officer he'd run into at the gas station. Jacobs tried to remember the officer's name and knew it was a common sounding name like Peeps, or Person, or, "Peoples! That's it," he thought, "Peoples!" He looked at the car as it drove away; wondering if there was anything to the coincidence. He thought about the detective until he reached his destination. When he greeted his friend, the name of the detective was still fresh on his tongue. The tech guy looked at the device and told Jacobs what he already knew, which wasn't helpful. "It's cheap and does the trick," he said. "Anyone can buy it and track it by a cell phone, or they can use a throw away phone so there's no trace. Yeah, I like it, thinking about putting one on Élan's car, are you?" Jacobs shook his head "No, no. Someone put it on my car." The tech friend looked surprised, and then he got serious as he watched Jacob's expression change. "Well, I can contact the company that sells them and let you know what I find out. I won't be able to get you a name or address of who bought it, but depending on what my contact knows, I can definitely get you more than what you know now." Jacobs looked at his friend and smiled. "Get me what you can as soon as you can. I can make sure whomever gives it up gets paid for their information." He left two hundred dollars on the counter and walked out.

As he returned to his car, Jacobs decided he needed to lay low for a while; his desire would have to be contained for the time being. He needed to put all his resources and time into trying to find out who put the tracking device on his car. The idea that someone had been following him made him nervous. He wondered how long the device had been on his car; was there one on Élan's car? It was more than he wanted to deal with. Was it the stripper he took to his building? No, it didn't make sense that she would do it. Besides, he thought, she wasn't that smart. Was it the small man, who met his fate on the other side of a door? No, it wasn't him. He knew the small man had been following him, and he knew why. The small man was disgruntled for sure, but a tracking device? No it couldn't be him. There were others he thought of but no one seemed capable or had a reason to know his whereabouts. He thought out loud as he drove home. Who would have a need to track his comings and goings? "Who?" he thought aloud, then he saw the face in his imagination; a detective, that's who! "Peoples! But why would he want to track me? What does he know, what has he found out, who has he spoken to," Jacobs asked himself as he drove home, trying to figure out why Peoples would put a tracking device on his car. When did he have a chance to place it? He would have to wait until his friend got back to him with information that he hoped answered his questions. As Jacobs pulled into his driveway, a car sat across the street watching him as he got out and went into his house.

UNDERSTANDING THE BEGINNING

Josey got out of the apartment without any problems. She began walking down the street without any idea of where she was headed. With no money or a phone, she knew she needed to find her way to the police station or to a shelter. As she continued, she noticed a group of ladies coming out of a drugstore and decided they looked friendly enough to ask for money. As she approached, one of the ladies stopped and asked her if she was okay. Josey was surprised because she didn't recognize the woman, but the way the lady spoke to her made her feel as if she was someone she should have known. "Honey, are you okay? I haven't seen you in years! Josey? Josey, don't you remember me?" She didn't remember the lady, but decided it didn't matter, because what she needed was to get away from where she was. The lady took her hand and guided Josey toward her car. "Get in baby; you look like you're in some trouble. I'll take you to my house; unless you got somewhere else you want me to me drop you off?" Josey shook her head no, and got in the car. As the two drove away, she asked the lady her name, "Brenda, don't you remember? We sang in the choir together way back when. Girl, you don't remember how we used to sing, you and me? Come on, now, surely you remember! I was the only one on your side when all that stuff came out about you and Huber right before he cancelled the wedding." Josey began remembering the woman, but she looked different. "Oh I know why you don't remember me; I lost over one hundred pounds, so I probably look a little different to you." That was it, Josey thought, the Brenda she remembered was very fat and round, this Brenda was very skinny. "I remember, she said, you look good Brenda!" "Thanks girl, yeah I had to lose that weight. I had weight loss surgery and I've kept it off for 3 years now. What about you, what you been up to? You look good, not as good as you used to look, but you look good; you've always been pretty. I guess that's why when they said you were born a man I didn't believe it, I mean, really?" Josey, smiled, thankful she had run into someone who knew her.

When they arrived at Brenda's house, Josey got out of the car, debating whether or not to tell her new/old friend where she had been for the last 2 weeks. She decided against it. She wanted to gain a sense of normality and needed to rest. Then, maybe, she'd tell her. Brenda told her to take off her shoes and get comfortable while she made them something to eat. She did as she was told and looked around her friend's house. She noticed several pictures, some of her friend when she was very heavy and some after the weight loss. She noticed a number of pictures of her friend singing. One in particular was of her in a choir. Brenda came in, carrying two bowls of salad and bottles of water. "Here you go, sweetheart." Josey took the bowl and asked her friend about the picture of the choir. "Oh yeah, you should remember that one, you were there when that was taken." Josey picked up the photograph and looked at it closely, trying to recognize faces. "Here, let me show you," her friend said. "Right here is me, the old me, that is. This one here is Julie, you remember her I bet; she was a real pistol," Brenda said, pointing in turn at each face. "This one is Marvin, and this one here is James. This one is Ronald, he had a crush on me way back then, can you believe it? We kind of dating right now, but he don't really like the new me, he liked me when I was heavy, ain't that something?" Brenda laughed. Josey smiled as she reminisced with her. "I know what! I got something you'd like. Stay right there, I'll be right back." Her friend returned with an envelope full of pictures, "Look at these, I bet you remember these."

Josey slowly pulled out picture after picture, remembering her days with the church, more importantly, her days with Huber. Then she saw one in particular, a picture of Huber. Her heart sank and her eyes watered. There were several pictures of herself and Huber together and there was one of Groves. Both she and Brenda growled when they saw the picture of Groves. They laughed at the emotion the picture produced and Brenda cursed. "Sorry, baby, but that man should have never been a pastor, he was just bad. Josey continued looking through the pictures until she came upon one that looked oddly familiar to her, "Brenda, who is this in this picture?" Brenda looked closely at the picture and rubbed her chin in thought. "Oh, that's the Mawabes. They were a family from Africa who moved here almost 20 years ago. They joined the church after that incident with their little girl. "What incident? What happened?" Josey asked.

"Well, from what I remember, their little girl was playing outside one Sunday morning with her dolls, you know, like a tea party. This guy comes by and is playing with her when her father comes out and sees him; he doesn't think anything about it. The guy leaves with the little girl, though, and does some nasty things to her. The father didn't pay much attention to the man and didn't realize until much later that the man had taken her; but by then the damage had already been done. That child was never the same after that and neither was the father. I heard she started doing drugs and stripping and stuff. I think she got killed, or died from a drug overdose or something; not really sure, but I know she's dead now." Josey stared at the picture as she listened to the story. "Brenda, did she have a brother?" Josey asked. "You know, I don't know, but it sure looks like it on that picture," Brenda replied. "There was a mother too, but she went back to Africa after it happened; actually, I think she took the boy with her." Josey reached into her purse, and pulled out the picture she had taken from the apartment. It was the same.

The phone rang as Jacobs headed toward his house, "Hello?" It was his tech friend. "Hey buddy, got some news for you. The tracking device was ordered online by someone who paid cash." Jacobs became enraged, and yelled into the phone, "Is that all you got? You called to tell me that, that's nothing! Why in hell did you call to tell me that bullshit?" "Calm down man, I got more, the techie answered, I know who tracked you." "Okay, who is it?" Jacobs asked. "It belongs to someone named Peoples. Does that make you happy?" Jacobs smiled broadly into the phone, and said, "Yes, yes, it makes me very happy. I'll stop by tomorrow and bring cash." He hung up the phone, and returned to his car. The driver sitting across the street started his car and followed.

Josey began to relax, and found herself enjoying the visit with her old friend. The two women laughed as they shared story after story about their time at the church. Pictures of certain people brought either tears or laugher and sometimes both. Josey was glad she was back in Kansas City, but more importantly she was glad to be away from her protector. She started to wonder if the child on the photograph was the man who had bathed, washed her hair and fed her for two weeks. She was almost positive it was him all grown up, but why did he rescue her? He didn't know her, she was certain of that. She looked at the picture again and thought about the child snatched away from her parents, and possibly molested. She imagined how different the child's life would have been had she remained safe with her parents and allowed to grow up free of harm. She knew what it was like to have your life changed in an instant, because it happened to her when Huber committed suicide. She knew what it was like to search for comfort through drugs, or do things other people thought disgusting because you felt you were worth nothing. She cried for the little girl lost, and she cried for herself. Brenda noticed the change in her demeanor and the tears in her eyes. "Sweetie what's wrong? Is there something I can do for you?" Josey shook her head as she got up and hugged her friend. "No, Brenda, but tomorrow there's something I need to tell you. For now, I'd just like to go to sleep." Brenda got up and gathered together a blanket and a pillow, "Couch or bed, you pick." Josey smiled and headed for the couch.

Josey awoke to the smell of coffee and scrambled eggs. Brenda sang as she prepared breakfast for her guest. As she called out to her friend, Josey was busy folding the blanket she used the night before. "Good morning sweetie," Brenda smiled, "how did you sleep?" "Wonderful," said Josie as she took her longtime friend's hand, "I can't begin to tell you how good it was to sleep on your sofa." "Well, let's get some food in us, because I bet you got a lot to do today." Brenda placed a plate in front of Josey and poured coffee into a large mug. The women sipped coffee, Then Josey began to speak. "Brenda, I need to share some things with you. For the last two weeks I've been kept by a man who took really good care of me. When he found me, I was lying on the ground, high on drugs and looking awful. This man rescued me and got me clean. He washed me, fed me and bought me clothes." Brenda was quiet as she listened to her friend. "He was my protector, but there was something strange about him. He never talked much, mostly read the Bible to me. Sometimes, after he'd receive a phone call he would leave and when he returned, he would be in a completely different mood. One time after he'd gotten one of those calls, he returned looking as if he had been in a fight; there were scratches on his arms. I never asked him about it because we didn't have that type of relationship. The whole time I was there I was afraid, because I didn't know what he would do. He never hit me or anything, but there was something about him that let me know he was not someone to challenge. When you found me yesterday, I had escaped. I waited for him to leave and I got the hell out of there. I didn't know where I was going or what I was going to do. Luckily, I ran into you." Brenda got up from the table and poured herself another cup of coffee; then she filled Josey's cup. "The other thing I need to tell you is that after Huber's death, I moved to Atlanta. I was a mess, Brenda; I turned tricks and got hooked on crack. It was a bad time for me. One time, I met a john who asked me to do some really strange things and right after that, I got on the next bus headed to KC. I spent one night with a guy who picked me up from the bus station after I asked him for money.

He bought me some food and let me stay the night. After that it was one night after another, until the man, the one I called my 'Protector', rescued me." Josey excused herself and returned with two pictures; the one she brought with her and the one of the family whose child had been taken. "Look at these pictures Brenda, what do you think? Is it the same family?" Brenda looked closely at both photographs, examining each face, looking for similarities. "Yes, it's the same picture," she said. Josey looked at the picture again, and told Brenda she thought the little boy on the picture was her benefactor.

Peoples was exhilarated and anxious as he headed to his car. He couldn't believe his luck, his only expectations when he visited the dancer was to find out about the building Jacobs had taken her to. To discover that Jacobs had taken tears from both her and Cindy, and that the small man who Cindy had been seen with knew Jacobs, was almost too much. He started the car and realized that he was close to arresting Jacobs. Now, he needed to compose himself as he examined the evidence. As he headed to the police station, his phone rang; Vhannie was calling. He paused, considering whether or not to answer the line. He was so close to catching Jacobs, he didn't want any distractions and answering Vhannie could get him off track. He let it ring, and soon she hung up. He pulled into police station parking and almost ran into the building.

Jacobs found Peoples' address after he discovered who'd been responsible for placing the GPS on his car. He wanted to visit the detective who had been watching him, now it was his turn to do the watching. He drove around the block several times looking out for nosy neighbors or a police officer on patrol. When he was sure no one had seen him, he parked his car and watched the house. He knew the type of car Peoples drove and quickly realized he wasn't home. There was another car parked in the driveway. It didn't matter; he was only interested in the detective, so he waited. Another car, unnoticed, parked across street, its driver watching Jacobs and hoping this was his opportunity to kill the monster. The man in the car who had acted as benefactor and 'Protector' also acted as vigilante. He watched Jacobs, allowing his anger to build as he fantasized about bullets ripping into Jacobs' body. He smiled at the thought of Jacobs' body, riddled with bullets, bringing peace to a family torn apart and avenging the death of his sister.

He knew Jacobs would never suspect that the small man he'd shot through a peep hole would have a son destined to avenge his murder. He was only 10 when Jacobs grabbed his sister and did horrible things to her. The incident tore the family apart. He and his mother returned to Africa, unable to remain in a country that would allow such a thing to happen to its children. His father was never the same as he raised his daughter alone; he did the best he could. He tried his best to keep his daughter's spirits high and her self-esteem intact. But as she got older, the hurt seemed to follow her and soon she found herself in a world of sex for money, and money for drugs. She danced at several gentlemen's clubs, but soon discovered her beauty was a burden instead of a blessing. The dancing paid her dealer and her bills; but her soul was void.

One night a group of men came to the bar and asked the manager if they could hire girls for a private party away from the club. Jacobs was with them. The girls overheard the request and recognized a few of the men as prominent clergy throughout the city. Since the men offered to pay above the normal rate for the girls the deal was done. The men engaged in sexual acts with the girls, determined to act out their wildest fantasies. One preacher in particular was determined to have her. He took her into another room and paid her to do things with him that he had only dreamed of doing. She did her job and got her money. As she was about to leave, Jacobs asked her to dance for him. She declined and asked that he schedule another time, she was tired. He gazed at her and smiled, remembering a small, brown, round faced little girl playing in her front yard with tea cups. He told her he didn't want to reschedule and offered her more money than ever. She consented. Then she remembered him as well, as he collected her last tear.

Peoples thought about calling Vhannie back, but decided against it. He sat at his desk and wrote down everything he thought important to the case against Jacobs. He wrote down the major players: Jacobs, the small man, Cindy, the stripper, Green BioChemicals, Levar, Kayla and Josey. What he already knew was that Jacobs was collecting tears from his victims, both young and old, and somehow turning them into fragrances. Cindy was killed by someone, Jacobs? Perhaps, but he wasn't sure. The small man found dead in his apartment was a friend of Jacobs, and Cindy's boyfriend. Jacobs was a pedophile and would attempt to grab another child if Peoples didn't stop him soon. His phone rang again. Again it was Vhannie. This time he answered.

As Josey and Brenda reminisced, she knew this was her last opportunity to change her life and get it right once and for all, so she continued to share with Brenda the things she had done. Brenda interrupted her once, as she recalled another incident she thought might be related to the man in the picture. "Josey, do you remember when Groves died? You know some people speculated he was killed by a jealous husband. He was such a cheat, and always trying to get in some woman's pants; who knows. But there was a rumor that he went to a strip club and had sex with that little girl who had been grabbed. She was all grown up by then, but when her father found out he confronted Groves." Josey listened attentively. She needed to purge another secret she'd kept hidden for years. "Yeah, I think Groves and that man got into a huge fight over the fact Groves had slept with the man's daughter. Unfortunately, he was no match for Groves, he was a small man and I think Groves got the best of him. They kept that quiet for a long time. His son knew about it though, and I think that man had something to do with Michael Groves' murder. Josey hadn't thought about Michael or his father for a long time. She was quiet as she poured her third cup of coffee. "Brenda, I feel so ashamed for what I'm about to tell you." Brenda looked at Josey and braced herself, "What is it?"

"After Huber died, I was so hurt and angry about the wedding being cancelled and the way Groves went after Huber, I decided to go after him. I always knew he was a whore, and he would never turn down a good lay, so I called him one night and asked him to come over. He did and within an hour he was in my bed telling me he wanted to have what Huber had. He had this thing for Huber, it was a constant competition, and he looked at me as just another thing to compete for, even though Huber was already dead. After it was over I felt dirty and stupid. Trying to get back at him was dumb; the only one who lost was me. I should have been satisfied trying to get back at Groves, but I wasn't, so I started trying to seduce Michael. He wasn't his father, and he never accepted my invitations. So I moved to Atlanta." Brenda looked at Josey with concern, and asked her if she was okay. "Yes, I'm okay, just had to get this off my chest. Thank you for listening." "Oh honey, that's what friends are for, but you know if you think the man who took care of you is the brother of the little girl who was grabbed so long ago, we need to go to the police." They drove in silence to the police station.

Vhannie told Peoples over the phone her thoughts regarding their last conversation. She told him she'd discovered someone who knew Jacobs and his buying habits. Jacobs bought scents that mimicked nature. He turned to Green Bio-Chemicals because they could recreate any scent he wanted. He placed custom orders, describing each scent in the most intricate details. The amount he requested was always small, but he demanded they send it in huge boxes. The person she spoke to at the company said he thought Jacobs was somewhat eccentric, but a good customer. The orders, he said, had been slow lately, he was not sure why. Peoples listened as he looked over the names he had written down. As he ended the call, he was informed he had visitors. The women were led to his desk where they began telling the story of the little girl who was stolen from her yard twenty years ago. Peoples looked at both women and then recognized one of them; "Josey? Is that you?"

The man watched Jacobs as he waited for Peoples to arrive. He opened a small briefcase he'd taken from his safe deposit box. Inside were hand-written notes from his father about Jacobs' comings and goings. The small man had been following Jacobs ever since his daughter started dancing at the club. He knew about the party where the city's most prominent clergy had engaged in unspeakable sexual fantasies. He knew his daughter left with Jacobs that night, and later her body was found in her apartment, where she'd chosen to end her pain by slashing her wrists. He followed

Jacobs, and kept detailed notes of each of Jacobs' grabs. He visited the club regularly after his daughter's death, trying to save each of the girls there one by one, but never succeeded. Then he met Cindy, and decided he would focus on her. She loved him the way a woman loves a man, he loved her as both the daughter he lost and as a woman. He tried to save her, but when Jacobs found out he had been following him, he shot the small man through his door. With her lover out of the picture, Cindy had no one to protect her. She subsequently took a ride with Jacobs that offered no return. The notes told everything; dates, times, places and even descriptions of what each child wore. The man in the car, Josey's 'Protector', read the notes, growing angrier with each word, each page. He stared at Jacobs' car and wondered how he would feel once he saw the life leave Jacobs' body.

Josey didn't know Peoples, but once he started telling her about the conversation he had with Jeanne, she understood why he recognized her. The women talked about the family who arrived in Kansas City and how they became a part of the church. They told him about the father who had lost a daughter, and the son who went back to Africa with his mother but had returned. Josey showed her pictures to Peoples and identified the young man on the picture as the man who had taken care of her for two weeks. She explained how the man found her on the streets and took extra care of her. Peoples looked at the picture and realized he had seen the same picture in the apartment of the small man who was shot through the door. He was beginning to connect the pieces together. Peoples asked Josey if the man in Atlanta who captured her tears was Jacobs, she said she didn't know his name, but if he had a picture she could id him. Peoples showed her a picture of Jacobs and she nodded in the affirmative.

The three talked for over an hour; Josey described her benefactor and Brenda offered truths and rumors about Huber and Groves, and who she thought killed Michael. Peoples realized the small man was the Cindy's boyfriend, and believed Jacobs had killed her. He also understood that the small man's son was now seeking revenge for his sister's plunge into drugs, and ultimately death. He knew Jacobs was responsible for most of the missing and exploited children in Kansas City within the last twenty years. He finally understood the connection to Green Bio-Chemicals; Jacobs wasn't making fragrances to stifle his urges, he was making them to remember his depraved acts. He knew why there were boxes at the non-descript building and why Jacobs took the stripper there; he was sure that was where the fragrances were made. Peoples needed to get a warrant to search the building but he wasn't sure if he'd be able to. Everything he knew was only a hunch and going to the DA with what he had would get the door slammed in his face. He still needed to catch Jacobs in the act, or he needed him to confess. He thanked the ladies and told them he'd keep in touch. He headed home.

Predator and prey were oblivious to each other. They were focused on their target and nothing or no one could distract them from it. Jacobs was thinking about his last attempt to grab a child and how a police car appeared after he was sure none had been present. He was sure Peoples had been behind it, especially after finding the GPS attached to his car. He hadn't thought about what he was going to do once the detective arrived, but he would make sure Peoples knew he was on to him. The man in the other car waited, wanting Jacobs to get out of his car, or better yet, he wanted Jacobs to attempt another grab, and then he would shoot him dead. He didn't care about being captured; his life had been nonexistent since his father was killed. The only bright moment he'd had in a long time had been finding and taking care of Josey. She never understood why he rescued her, but he knew she had been exploited and misused by Jacobs as well. His father had documented it all. He also knew whose house he sat in front of; it belonged to Detective Peoples. He wondered if Jacobs knew, or was he there waiting to grab an innocent little boy or girl whose life would be changed forever. His father had been to this house and in the woods where he was chased by a dog. He had seen Peoples at the ceremony, and watched him as he followed Jacobs. He wasn't sure how Peoples connected to Jacobs, but in the world in which he lived, no one was without suspicion.

When Peoples left the station, his plan was to go straight home, but his gut told him to go to the building where Jacobs made his fragrances. He was sure he'd be able to get in, plus he needed stronger evidence to put this predator away. If he couldn't get the front door open, he'd go through the back door; either way he was going to get in. As he neared the building he got a sudden urge to call Vhannie. He dismissed the feeling and proceeded to exit the car. He went to the back of the building and turned the doorknob, for some reason he expected the door to open, but it didn't. The area behind the building had been cleaned, all the boxes had been removed, and as he looked for something to get the door opened, he realized he was not good at breaking and entering. He paused, allowing himself time to think of a plan. He fished into his pocket hoping for a safety pin or something he could use to jimmy the lock. The only thing he found was a piece of gum, so he popped that in his mouth. He walked around the other side of the building hoping to find a way in, when he realized someone was watching him.

The young man asked Peoples if he needed help, he looked surprised and bemused as he realized the situation he was in. He had to think quickly to keep things from getting out of control. As he looked the young man over, he quickly assumed he was a thug and had probably broken into the building before. Yeah, you ever been in here, know how to get in? The young man darted around the side of the building and opened the door from the inside. The two went in, both going in opposite directions. Peoples didn't know what he would find; only that he would find what he needed to get Jacobs off the streets. He knew there was a room with beakers, test tubes, containers, cabinets and all kinds of things found in a chemistry lab; the stripper had described the room and he had to find it. The young thug had gone his own way as if he knew his way around the building. Suddenly Peoples heard a loud crash, and followed the sound to find the young man in the chemistry lab. He smiled thinking to himself he should have followed his co-conspirator in the first place. He had been in the building many, many, times before.

He looked through the first cabinet and found empty vials, nothing incriminating. He kept looking until he stumbled upon a book, detailing the many ways to make fragrances. As he read the book, he noticed the word 'Innoscents' Peoples soon understood what Vhannie had discovered, what Jacobs's disturbed mind had been concocting, and why he collected his victims' tears. In black and white he understood the degree of Jacobs' madness.

Vhannie paced back and forth anticipating Peoples arrival. She looked at Stank and remembered she had forgotten to feed him, so she grabbed the dry food and then she looked for his favorite canned beef. The pantry was empty except for a can of tuna, which Stank hated. She smiled at him and decided to go out and get a couple cans of beef. She figured Peoples would be home by the time she returned. She hesitated for a moment, debating whether or not to take him with her. She decided against it, and headed out the door.

The two men watched from across the street as she climbed into her car. Jacobs didn't recognize her, but it didn't matter, she was somebody Peoples knew and probably loved, so he followed her. As she pulled out of the drive way, he tailed her; the man in the other car was close behind. The three drove down several blocks until they reached the highway. Vhannie, completely unaware she was being followed, turned south onto the highway. Her only concern was getting back by the time Peoples arrived home. As she turned into the store's parking lot, her phone buzzed; it was Peoples. "Hi baby, what are you doing?" "I'm at the grocery store, about to get Stank some food. What are you doing?" People's voice was barely audible as he described what he found in Jacobs' building. Vhannie listened and began to cry, not only at what Peoples said, but at what she knew it was doing to him. "Baby, I'm on my way home, please get here quick. I've got to get that bastard and it's got to be tonight." "Yes," she said, "I'll be right there."

As she headed toward the door's entrance, she felt uneasy, and then noticed a large man in a black Ford Explorer staring at her. He was parked a few cars down from her in the aisle facing her. She continued on into the store. Once inside, she called Peoples again and asked what kind of car Jacobs drove. He told her it was a black Ford Explorer, but it could be a Honda Accord; it belonged to his wife and he sometimes drove it. Vhannie told him she thought Jacobs was outside the store and that he had been watching her. Peoples asked which store was she at and ended the call. He drove like a mad man, thinking Jacobs had followed her and fearing the worst. He drove so fast, he almost missed the Explorer as it pulled out of the parking lot. He had to think fast; follow Jacobs, or try to locate Vhannie. He decided to follow the Explorer.

There was another car following Jacobs, but Peoples hadn't noticed it. The buzz of his phone startled him as he pursued Jacobs. Vhannie's voice on the other end brought him back to reality and made him slow down. "Where are you?" she said. "Baby, get back to the house and lock the doors until I get there; I got this son of a bitch in my path and tonight he's going to jail." The Explorer took an exit onto a quiet street. Jacobs hadn't planned on doing anything to Vhannie; he only wanted to scare her and he knew when she recognized him she'd call Peoples. He saw the detective pull into the parking lot and turn to follow him. He wondered how long it would be before Peoples pulled him over. He knew Peoples didn't have anything on him and, since the GPS had been removed, he hadn't been able to track his movements. In addition, he hadn't tried to grab any children since the boy at the party. He drove along the street, waiting for the detective to stop him. Peoples continued to follow Jacobs as he realized he didn't have anything on the pervert. He couldn't call a fellow cop and have him cited again for expired plates, what could he do?

Jacobs knew the cat-and-mouse game was almost over. He stopped his car, turned off the engine, and watched Peoples do the same. The man in the third car pulled over to the opposite side of the street, exited his vehicle, and pulled out his gun as he approached Jacobs' Explorer. Peoples realized then that Jacobs was himself being followed, even as he tailed Vhannie, and wondered if the man approaching Jacobs was the same man Josey had described. He pulled out his service revolver, and began to exit his vehicle. Just then, a slow-moving blue van pulled alongside Jacobs' truck. From the passenger side, a child pointed a finger out the window at the large man in the black Explorer. Peoples saw a flash of light as the bullet exploded into the driver's side window, hitting Jacobs fully in the face. He watched smoke rise from the pavement as the van screeched away. The third man returned to his automobile. Moments later, he got out and walked over to Peoples car, handed him the book of notes, returned to his vehicle, and drove away.

Peoples looked at the notes and began to read

www.ingramcontent.com/pod-product-compliance
Lightning Source LLC
LaVergne TN
LVHW050634100826
845148LV00011B/1858

* 9 7 8 0 6 1 5 7 8 9 0 0 2 *